COVER GIRL

Mom had no way of knowing I'd never told Greg the truth—she naturally assumed I'd told the world about my new career.

"I'm not interested in hearing your excuses," Greg shouted. "All that matters is that you lied to me! Whatever happened to our trust?"

I'd never heard him raise his voice before, and the sound was harsh and ugly. "Nothing's happened," I said, "I love you, Greg."

"How do I know that? Here you are, obviously leading a secret life that you didn't want me to know about. How do I know you're not hiding anything else from me? I just don't trust you anymore."

Even from where I stood I could hear the slam of the front door. Numbly I walked over to the full-length mirror on the back of my bedroom door. "I hate you," I spat at the image before me. "I hate being pretty. I wish I was ugly." Then I turned and threw myself across my bed, sobbing uncontrollably.

Bantam Sweet Dreams Romances
Ask your bookseller for the books you have missed

Cover Girl

Yvonne Greene

BANTAM BOOKS
TORONTO • NEW YORK • LONDON • SYDNEY

RL 6, IL age 11 and up

COVER GIRL
A Bantam Book / February 1982

10 printings through December 1983

Cover photo by Pat Hill

ISBN 0-553-24323-3

Published simultaneously in the United States and Canada

Bantam Books are published by Bantam Books, Inc. Its trademark, consisting of the words "Bantam Books" and the portrayal of a rooster, is Registered in U.S. Patent and Trademark Office and in other countries. Marca Registrada. Bantam Books, Inc., 666 Fifth Avenue, New York, New York 10103.

PRINTED IN THE UNITED STATES OF AMERICA

O   19   18   17   16   15   14   13   12   11   10

Cover Girl

Chapter One

When I was six years old, I spent a lot of time dreaming about becoming a ballerina. I guess a lot of girls must have had that dream, at least judging by the number of other six-year-olds who used to crowd into Mrs. Anderson's studio every Saturday morning for lessons. I remember how excited I was on the first day of class and how grown up I felt dressed in my pink leotard and tights. But after months of trying to force my feet into the number two position without much success, I begged my mother to let me stop taking lessons.

Besides, I'd found a new goal: I was going to be a great actress, a movie star. I thought it would be terrific to be able to go to the movies with my girlfriends and then watch their mouths hang open as they discovered me smiling at them from the screen. But that dream died, too, after I messed up my five

1

lines at my church's Christmas play that year.
I just wasn't cut out to be an actress, either.

Then when I was seven, I decided I was
going to be a fashion model. Actually it wasn't
all my decision: a number of people, from the
mailman to the clerk in the shoe store, had
convinced my mother that my cute, whole-
some-looking face belonged in print. For a
while I practiced walking around the house
with a book on my head. But that fantasy
faded away after several New York agencies
told my mom that my dark hair and slightly
freckled face were not what they were looking
for. Although my mother seemed heartbroken
by the news, I wasn't upset at all; I was more
interested in playing with my friends.

Now that I was a junior in high school—
Eastbrooke High in Eastbrooke, New Jersey,
to be exact—I was beginning to get interested
in being a writer. My English teacher, Mrs.
Milton, had seen a spark of talent in my
writing and was pushing me to develop it.
She had encouraged me to write down all my
thoughts in a journal and wanted me to enter
the Nationwide Amateur Writing Contest in
the spring.

I even had Mrs. Milton to thank for getting
me together with Greg, the boy of my (pardon
the expression) dreams.

I used to think all boys were part of some

strange species that had nothing to do with human beings. Then when I finally realized they were people after all, I wasn't able to talk to them without stuttering or blushing or forgetting what I was going to say. My mom thought my shyness with boys probably had something to do with the fact that my father had died when I was four. She may have been right, I don't know. All I know is that I was afraid to talk to them.

But in tenth grade boys started talking to me—mostly, I guess, because I was considered pretty. At first I felt awkward, but after a while I found it was very much like talking to girls, although there were some topics I wouldn't *dare* talk about with a boy. A couple of guys even asked me out on dates. I had a good time but I could have had just as much fun with my girlfriends Marilyn or Julie. No matter how hard I tried, I just wasn't interested.

Except in Greg. He sat about four seats in front of me in English. I had watched him since the start of the school year. But no matter how often I stared at his earlobe or did other equally dumb things to try and make him notice me, he never did. Then when he finally would look in my direction, I'd blow the chance by looking away at the last minute.

When Mrs. Milton's class got really good,

however, I forced myself to stop staring at Greg's earlobe and get to work. I really wanted to be good enough to enter the writing contest, and I didn't want to blow the whole thing over a boy.

My best friend, Marilyn Underwood, suggested I ask *him* out. "Look, times have changed, Renée. How do you know he's not waiting for you to make the first move? How do you know *he's* not shy?"

She had a point. All this time, I had just assumed since he was good looking—with streaky blond hair that seemed to glow—and always had the right answers in class, that he was as outgoing as other boys I knew. Then I remembered when I'd run into him in the halls a couple of times and he had looked like he wanted to say something but ended up muttering only a hello before hurrying off. Maybe he *was* interested—and just afraid.

So I decided I would do it—I would ask him out. Anything was better than staring at the back of his head, waiting for him to notice me.

The day I picked was the day Mrs. Milton gave us an English exam. As soon as I sat down, I got to work, only looking up for a second when Greg walked in. First pass the test, then ask Greg out, I told myself. Hurriedly I returned my attention to the test booklet.

"How did you do?" Mrs. Milton asked when I turned in the exam toward the end of the class. She was especially concerned because this was a standardized test, and she had no control over its contents.

"Fine," I answered. "I'm sure I got my ten points for the writing essay. Now if I just got everybody's birthdays right and the number of poems they wrote, I'm all set."

Mrs. Milton sighed and looked around the room with her sharp, dark eyes. "Most students would rather memorize a bunch of facts than understand a good story," she said. "Usually they're the ones I worry about, but now I'm concerned about you and a couple of the others. These exams have no bearing on your true reading, writing, and comprehensive abilities. Maybe instead of teaching you how to understand literature, I should just give you a list of authors at the beginning of the year, complete with their birth dates and death dates and the titles of their works."

"Mrs. Milton," I said, "this class means a lot to me. I'd never have started liking Dickens or Austen if it hadn't been for you—not to mention the fact that I would've never known I could write."

Mrs. Milton's eyes softened just a bit. "If all my students were just a little more like you," she said, smiling, "I would believe I was in Utopia." Then, straightening up, she looked at me seriously. "Now, how's that essay coming along? The contest is less than two months away, and I want to submit the work of all my best students."

"I've started three different ones, but I can't get into any of them," I said.

"I've been thinking," Mrs. Milton went on. "Greg Neill has a wonderful sense of imagery but has trouble developing his ideas. You have a good sense of form but have problems with your imagery. I wonder if it wouldn't be good for the two of you to get together and compare notes? A little teamwork would help both of you."

I hoped Mrs. Milton wouldn't notice me blushing. It didn't help that at that very moment Greg walked forward to hand in his exam. If Mrs. Milton intended to pair us up now, in front of the whole class, I think I would have died.

Luckily she didn't. I tiptoed back to my seat and waited for the bell to ring. I saw Mrs. Milton talking to Greg, but I didn't want to stare. I looked down at my desk and thought about asking him out. At least now I would have a reason—he couldn't say no to something that was class-related, could he? Still, I was so nervous I was practically shaking.

I nearly tripped over my seat in my hurry to catch up to Greg when the class let out. He seemed to be caught up in a world of his own as he entered the hall, and as I was searching my brain for something to say to him, he smacked his head and whispered under his breath, "Now!"

"Now what?" I answered back, hoping he wouldn't be mad at me for breaking into his thoughts.

He looked my way and smiled. "Oh, hi, Renée," he said haltingly. He walked a few more steps, then as if apologizing, added, "I was just thinking about the test. Remember the question: name six major works by Jane Austen? During the test I could remember only five. I just now remembered the sixth."

"Yeah," I agreed. "It's really hard to remember titles if you haven't read the books."

Greg stared at me. I knew I had caught him unaware, but I didn't want to scare him off. Just to be sure, I pretended to rummage through my bag so he would have time to compose himself or whatever he needed to do. Maybe *I* needed to do it, too.

"I bet you read all her books," he said.

"Yeah," I admitted. "But Jane Austen is kind of a girls' writer anyway." I just made this up because I didn't know what else to say. Besides, I was too busy thinking about how nice his face looked close up. Even though it was early March, his face was getting tan. I knew that he spent a lot of time outdoors, and I wondered what it would be like to swim with him in a cool lake as blue as his eyes or climb a sunny mountain the same shade as his green flannel shirt.

"She is not," Greg said.

"Who isn't what?"

"Jane Austen isn't a girls' writer. I happen to love *Pride and Prejudice*. It's just when it comes to facts during exams that I'm not too good. I would've done a lot better with essay questions."

"Me, too!" I agreed. "In fact, Mrs. Milton was worried about us. She thought the exam would pull our grades down."

"You couldn't pull your grades down with a tow truck," Greg said.

"How do you know?" I said. I didn't know whether to be happy or annoyed to find out he'd been keeping track of my grades.

By now all the classes had let out, and we were surrounded by other kids. They jostled Greg and me from all sides, and finally we had to let the flow of bodies just carry us on down the hall. With all the laughing and shouting around us, talking to Greg became real easy. I wondered why I had waited so long to do it.

"Wow!" Greg exclaimed. "You hardly even have to walk when it gets this crowded. Just grab the people next to you and float along to your next class."

"What if you're going in the opposite direction?" I shouted in response, but I took the opportunity to clutch Greg's arm. I couldn't believe I had done that. He looked surprised, too, but then he smiled. By now our shoulders were pressed together, too, and it felt real good to be so close to him. I wondered if I'd ever get a chance to reach over and kiss him. Just thinking about it made my heart pound faster.

"Well, you never told me," I persisted, trying to keep the conversation going. "How do you know about my grades?"

"I sit in front of you," he replied. "So when I pass the papers back, I see the marks."

"That's not fair. I'm in back, and I don't get to spy on anybody's grades." I pretended to pout.

"You should sit up front with me," Greg said. I thought I saw him blush faintly. As if to cover up his remark, he added quickly, "I mean—Mrs. Milton says—I—uh—you—it would be helpful if we got together to work on our essays."

By the way he spoke, I knew he hadn't intended to bring it up just yet—just as I hadn't intended to agree so easily and so quickly. "That would be a great idea!" I blurted out.

This was working out very well, I thought. I might not have to ask him out, after all; he might ask me, instead.

"Yes," Greg continued. "She said you're great on style, and I'm poor on form."

"No, no!" I laughed. "You're great at creating images, and I'm lousy at it!"

There was an awkward pause, then Greg asked, "Well—so how about tonight?" He looked at me hesitantly.

"Great. You can pick me up any time after seven!" I said without missing a beat. "My mother and I eat around six-thirty, but I should be ready by then."

Greg looked at me dumbly. "Pick you up?" he repeated faintly. "I—I thought I'd come over to your place or something, and we could work on the essays there."

"Of course," I quickly corrected myself. "I forgot—the library's not open at night anymore. It's my house, then."

The thirty-second bell rang just then, and I hurried off to class. But then I remembered something and ran back to where Greg still stood in the hall.

"I forgot to give you my address," I gasped. "Oh, I know—1318 John Street." And then he blushed. I guess he was a lot better at facts than he wanted me to know.

Chapter Two

I hurried home that afternoon, jumped into the shower, and then spent the next three hours making myself look nice for Greg. Admittedly I was blessed with good looks, but I wanted to look really great. I put on black eyeliner to make my eyes stand out and brushed on lots of blush to make my cheeks glow. Usually I never bothered with makeup, but this was a special occasion.

Anyone looking at the bathroom could tell I was a beginner at it. My makeup was scattered all over the bathroom vanity along with half-a-box-worth of tissues stained with my many attempts at applying the eyeliner. I wished I'd listened all the times my mother had pestered me about learning how to use makeup. Still, messy as it was, I felt I was doing a reasonable job on myself.

"What's going on here?" Mom asked in

amazement when she came home from work.

Her sudden entrance made me smear my lipstick halfway down my chin. "Oh, hi, Mom. Sorry about the mess. I'll clean it up—"

"That's okay," she said. "I'm glad to see you finally taking an interest in your looks. Must be a boy, right?"

I looked at her oddly. "How'd you know?"

Mom smiled. "Why else would you bother? Just hurry it up in here. Dinner will be ready in ten minutes."

As we ate I filled Mom in on Greg. Although she seemed glad a boy was coming over, I could tell she was preoccupied with something else. She didn't say much and kept glancing at the phone as if she were willing it to ring. Sure enough, shortly before seven it did. She ran for it, picking up the receiver before the second ring.

Maybe it has something to do with a new job, I hoped. I knew Mom was miserable with her job as a secretary in a plastics company, especially since she had been passed up for a promotion several months earlier.

I didn't have time to think about it, however, for Greg rang our doorbell exactly at seven. Mom was still on the phone and nodded pleasantly in his direction as I led him through the hallway into the living room.

"I brought what I've written so far," Greg

14

said after he sat down on the sofa. "I thought maybe you could read my stuff while I read yours, and then we could take turns going over each of them."

"I still haven't decided on a topic, and all I have right now are some scribbled notes. Maybe you can make some sense out of them." I handed him my note pad as he gave me a folder filled with cleanly typed sheets. Our fingers touched briefly, causing me to tingle inside.

The room was silent as we pored over each other's work. Greg had written a long, detailed account about the joys of hiking alone in the woods. I thought it was well written; he had a way of making the woods come alive. I felt as if I were standing right in the middle of them.

"I don't know what Mrs. Milton was talking about," I said after I'd finished it. "I think your writing's excellent."

"Thanks, Renée," he said, blushing. "But there are lots of problems with it. I kind of go from one image to another without really tying them together."

"But they're so beautiful!"

"That's because I've picked a subject I know a lot about—the outdoors and the environment. It's a good theme for an essay, but the writing's not good enough for the contest. It still needs a lot of work."

"I'd like to help," I said. "That is, if you'll let me."

"That's why I'm here," he replied. "I've always thought you were a good writer, and I'm glad Mrs. Milton suggested we do this. I—I'd never have had the nerve to ask you on my own."

"Why not?"

Greg paused, as if he were searching for the right words to say. "I—I don't know. I guess I always figured a girl like you would be unapproachable. But you're not—unapproachable, that is. You're easy to talk to."

"That's funny, Greg. I thought the same thing about you."

"You did? Look at all the time we've wasted!"

I couldn't help laughing, for I was thinking the same exact thing. "Good. Now that we've got that out of the way, we can get back to work," I said, still laughing a little.

Greg picked up my note pad. "I think I know why you're having trouble with your essay," he said. "It's the topics you've picked. Like this one." He pointed to one page. "What do you really know about 'our military preparedness?' No offense, but what you've got here sounds like something that was written by a high school junior who's researched what somebody else said in the newspapers.

16

I'm no expert, but I think you might be more comfortable writing about something that you've actually experienced."

"You really think so?" I was upset at hearing Greg's criticism, but deep down I suspected he might be right. "But I haven't done much of anything."

"Sure you have. You're a bright girl, you're beautiful. You must have done lots worth writing about."

I couldn't believe he had said that. He seemed surprised, too.

I looked down and shrugged. "Maybe," I said. "I don't know. But I tell you what. Since your essay's farther along than mine, why don't we work on it first? That way, at least one of us will have something solid to submit to the contest."

"Sounds good. I like a person who gets right to the point."

"Me, too. I think I'm going to like working with you." I hoped he read the meaning behind my words.

He smiled. "Great. By the way, how much do you know about the outdoors? It would help if you knew something about it."

"A little," I answered truthfully. "I was a Girl Scout for a little while, but to tell you the truth, I haven't done much camping since then. My mom thinks that girls shouldn't go off into the woods alone." I gave him one of those you-know-mothers looks.

"Actually your mom's right," Greg said. "It can be pretty dangerous to go off on your own."

"Still, she tends to be overprotective of me. . . ."

"I've got an idea. Do you think she'd let you go hiking with an escort? I'm going up to Bear Lake on Saturday with two of my cousins and their girlfriends, and you're welcome to join us if you like."

"I'd love to," I said. "What time?"

"Oh, about nine. And Renée?"

"Yes?"

"I don't want you to think I'm inviting you just so you can help me with the essay. So—would you like to go to the movies with me tomorrow night?"

"Yes, I would."

"Good, I was hoping you'd say that." He looked at me shyly. "I'm really not good at playing games. I prefer to deal openly with people. What I mean is—uh—I like you, Renée."

"I'm glad, Greg, 'cause I like you, too."

We looked at each other intently, savoring the meaning of what we'd just told each other.

"I hope you don't mind, then, if I ask a favor of you," he said a bit hesitantly. "Do you mind not putting all that stuff on your face when we go out?"

I was stunned momentarily. "You mean my makeup?"

"I think you look pretty without it," he said. "I guess I like the natural look. I hope I haven't upset you."

I smiled sheepishly. "No, you haven't, Greg. As a matter of fact, you've just freed me from hours of slaving in front of the bathroom mirror. I'd just as soon not be bothered. Most boys would expect me to do that for them, but I'm kind of glad you don't."

"It's just something I've never liked," he explained. "I just think that all that makeup puts a barrier between two people. It can hide the real person underneath."

"I'm glad you told me. It's better to be up front about these things, don't you think?"

"I'm all for honesty—it's the best policy."

I winced. "Oh, Mrs. Milton would get you for that one. 'Cliché,' she'd yell."

"You're right," he said, grinning. "I'd better work on my descriptions. Speaking of working, I think I'd better get home. I've still got the rest of my homework to do. Thanks for letting me come over."

"Thank *you*, Greg—for everything," I said, walking him to the door. "See you tomorrow."

After I let Greg out, I walked dreamily to the

kitchen to grab a snack. Greg was unlike any other boy I'd known, but it was a difference I liked. Already I felt as if we were old friends, free to joke and laugh and even criticize each other.

I'd poured myself a glass of milk and was just about to reach for the box of chocolate chip cookies on the counter when Mom suddenly appeared in the kitchen doorway.

"Renée, put those cookies down," she practically shouted. "I've got to talk to you."

"What's the matter, Mom?" I asked, sitting down at the table.

Mom sat across from me, looking like she was about to burst. "I didn't want to interrupt you—oh, you're not going to believe—you'll have to cut out the cookies for a while—oh, I don't know where to begin—"

"What is it, Mom? Does it have something to do with the phone call earlier?"

Mom composed herself. "This isn't going to make any sense to you unless I start at the beginning. Do you remember when that photographer came by a few months ago?"

I remembered. Mom had hired him to take photos for Dad's relatives in California. The shaggy-haired man took only a few shots of Mom and me. The rest were all of me—sitting on a rock, leaning against a tree, smiling off into the sunset. It got pretty boring after a while, and I found myself wondering if Dad's family really would be interested in having a hundred or so photos of the niece, cousin, or granddaughter they hardly even knew.

"Yeah, what about it?"

"I wasn't totally honest about it. The photos weren't for the relatives. They were for a modeling agency."

"You mean you sent my photos to a modeling agency? Why didn't you tell me? What for?"

"I didn't want to disappoint you," she said. "In case you were rejected. But you weren't, honey. The agency has accepted you, and they want to see you tomorrow!" Mom was beaming as if she'd just won the jackpot at Atlantic City.

I was simply in shock—it was too much to believe. "You mean to model? They want *me* to model?"

"That's right," Mom said.

"But how could they accept me without seeing me?"

"They fell in love with your pictures. It seems you have exactly what they're looking for. The market today is flooded with blondes, and all the clients are tiring of them. The head of Photo Star told me she went crazy over your long, dark hair. It's one of your greatest selling points."

"Did you say Photo Star? But that's one of the top agencies in New York!" I had read about them in one of the teen magazines. The importance of what she was saying was starting to sink in.

"That's what I've been trying to tell you," Mom cried, sounding like a little girl. "They love your looks and think you can have a great future as a model. Isn't it exciting?"

"I—I don't know what to say. It's all so sudden. . . . "

Mom looked at me sympathetically. "I guess it is quite a shock for you." Then, glancing at the clock, she added, "We'll talk more in the morning. I want you to run off to bed now. You've got a big day ahead of you tomorrow."

Suddenly I thought of Greg and our date. "What time will we get back from New York? Greg's asked me out for tomorrow night."

"Greg?" Mom asked as if she had never heard of him. "Oh, the boy. I guess you'll be back in time for your date."

"Good." I couldn't believe what was happening. If what Mom said was true, by tomorrow night I'd be a full-fledged model!

Chapter Three

Wiping the sleep from my eyes, I faced my bowl of cornflakes the next morning. Despite Mom's orders I had hardly slept at all. I had lain in bed, wide awake, thinking over and over what it would be like to pose for photographers all over New York. I tried to imagine seeing myself in fashion layouts and advertisements—even on the cover of a big magazine! When I finally forced myself to stop thinking about all that, my thoughts shifted to Greg. It was close to three before I drifted off to sleep.

"Are you feeling all right, honey?" Mom broke into my thoughts. Dressed in a very businesslike gray herringbone suit, she was busily making me tuna salad for lunch. That image of her looking so nice while hunched over the kitchen counter struck me as out of sync, sort of like how the president of the United States might look taking out the garbage. I'd told her often enough that I could make my own lunch or even pick up some lunch at school, but she insisted on making it. Deep down inside, I had to admit I liked her lunches anyway, although lately she'd stopped putting in the little surprises I liked, such as chocolates from the office or her homemade banana cake. "Too fattening," she had said when I'd asked her about it. Now I knew why.

"I'm okay," I replied, looking up from the cereal bowl. The sound of the crunchy flakes in my head as I chewed helped wake up my overtired brain cells.

"Don't tell me you're okay," my mother persisted. "You look pale and drawn. Didn't you sleep well last night?"

"Sure," I lied, but then on second thought, I added, "I slept perfectly well while I was sleeping. I just happened to stay up most of the night."

"But *why*!" my mother gasped. "I told you to get your sleep." From the way she reacted, you would have thought I'd just admitted to robbing a bank.

"I was thinking about today, that's why."

"Renée Renshaw!" was my mother's unexpectedly annoyed reply. "Now that you'll be modeling you have to have some respect for

24

your body. Look at your pretty face. It's all gray and pasty." She sounded as if she had awakened on the wrong side of the bed. Maybe she hadn't slept much, either.

Trying to look down at my face, I crossed my eyes. But all I could see was the tip of my nose. Two tips, as a matter of fact, and both very much out of focus.

But making faces didn't improve Mom's mood. "Stop making cross-eyes at me," she complained. "I have the right to be concerned. I'm your mother, remember? That's the last late night for you." To herself she added, "I should have waited till this morning to tell you."

"Okay," I agreed, trying to sound pleasant. I hoped this modeling business wouldn't turn her into a nervous wreck.

Getting up from the table, I put my dishes in the sink and looked for my books. "Gotta go now. I'll come home from school as fast as I can."

"Okay," Mom said. "Don't mind me. I'm just worried about this afternoon." She bent over her coffee cup reading the morning paper, her elbows anchored on the table, and from where I stood, I could detect three gray strands in her otherwise dark hair. For some reason I thought of my father just then, and I wondered how he'd feel about his daughter being a model. Then I wondered whether he would've been gray by now, or maybe even going bald. It was hard to imagine him any other way than the way he looked in the photograph on my mother's dresser. To us, he would always be twenty-eight years old and smiling under a thick mop of dark hair.

I was just about to say goodbye when Mom spoke again. She didn't actually look up from her coffee cup, so I was never quite sure it was me she was talking to. She just kind of mumbled, as if she were speaking to herself more than to me. "You know, when I was your age, I looked a lot like you. The same tall, slim figure, the long, dark hair—even the face, though you have your father's brown eyes. Then I met Daddy, and you came along, and . . . " Her voice drifted off a bit so I couldn't quite hear the rest—not that I really wanted to. I worried that if I hung around any longer I was going to be late for school, and besides, Mom's nostalgic moods of late made me just a little nervous. Grabbing my books, I blew her a hasty kiss and made off for school.

When I got to biology class after lunch, Mr. Brooks, my teacher, handed me a note from the principal's office. It read: *Renée Renshaw,*

call your mother at work immediately.
Naturally I got a little scared. Mom had been awfully tense at breakfast. Maybe the agency didn't want me after all!

The hall looked dark and eerily quiet as I stepped out into it. Just minutes before, hundreds of shouting and shrieking kids had pushed and shoved their way through it to classes all over the building. Now there wasn't a trace of anyone.

A lone pen lay discarded on the scuffed hall floor. I bent down to pick it up and used it to dial my mother's number at work at the pay phone at the end of the hall. As I dialed, I noticed that somebody had written Greg and Mary in bright red ink over the face of the phone. I froze for a moment, the way I always did when I saw his name or heard it spoken. But I knew this wasn't the same Greg. If there was a Mary, I would've known by now.

"Stanford Plastics," said a cheerful voice at the other end of the line.

"Is Brit Renshaw there, please?" I asked. "This is her daughter, Renée."

"Why, Renée, how are you?" the voice answered back. "This is Mrs. Rolly—remember me? Maggie."

"Of course I do, Mrs. Rolly," I answered politely. "Is my mother there? I got an urgent message to call her, and I just wondered—"

"You see what happens," Maggie chatted on, totally oblivious to the panic in my voice. "It's such a strange world. One day you meet a pretty little girl at your co-worker's Christmas party—"

"Mrs. Rolly!" I nearly shouted into the mouthpiece. "I've got to speak to my mother. It's an *emergency*!" A classroom door near me suddenly slammed shut and made me jump in surprise.

"Why, of course, dear," Maggie agreed calmly. "She's right here."

"Hi, dear," I heard Mom say. "I'm so glad you called back so quickly."

"Is everything all right?" I asked her anxiously.

"Of course. I just wanted to let you know the appointment's been confirmed for four."

"Is that all? I thought something terrible had happened."

"I also wanted to remind you to wash your hair," she continued, as if reading off a list.

"It's clean, Mom," I said. "I washed it yesterday."

"Not clean enough. It has to sparkle. Renée, don't give me a hard time—just do as I say, okay?"

"Yes, Mom," I replied.

"And put on some mascara and blush-on,

too. You looked like a ghost this morning. Do you still look tired?"

"I don't know. I haven't checked." Maybe that sounded snide, but I was hurt that she asked me if I looked tired. How about whether I *felt* tired? Didn't she understand how this news was affecting me?

"Really, honey, it's unnatural! Most girls your age spend *hours* in front of the mirror. Thank goodness the agency saw the potential. . . ."

A teacher from a nearby classroom stuck his head out the door to check the large hall clock hanging overhead. I followed his gaze and noticed the time. I had to get back to biology class; I was behind in lab work as it was.

"Mom, I gotta go. I'm supposed to be in class."

"Don't worry. You do well enough in school. But never mind—I'll see you at home at three. And remember, you don't have time to spend with Marilyn and Julie today. And put on a nice outfit. I'm afraid that until you're an established model, you won't get away with wearing blue jeans."

"Okay."

"And makeup. 'Bye, dear." With that the phone clicked silent, and I returned to my class. Boy, I thought, returning to my lab experiment, if being a model is going to mean taking orders from Mom like a robot, it's not going to be much fun at all. . . .

Chapter Four

Marilyn came home with me after school, even though I told her she wasn't supposed to. But how do you keep your best friend from following you onto a public bus and sitting next to you on the seat?

"I have to come with you and help you dress," she insisted after we fell giggling onto the long seat in the back of the bus. I usually walked home from school, it being only fifteen minutes away, but today I was in a hurry. I figured if I was lucky, the bus could save me five minutes, leaving me more drying time for my hair.

In eighth grade, kids started calling Marilyn and me Mutt and Jeff because of the way we looked next to each other. We both hated it. Still, even at sixteen, the names fit. No matter how Marilyn tried, she could never shed the extra ten pounds that made her chunky, while I could never gain the ten pounds I needed to stop being skinny. We had both grown two inches in the last year, but she was still short, and I was still tall. To add to our differences, Marilyn was what you would call a "pert blonde," while people thought of me as a "serious brunette." I always kind of liked that image of me, while Marilyn had convinced herself a long time ago that "blondes have more fun."

"So why do you have to go to the agency if they already accepted you?" Marilyn asked when we got off the bus and jogged down one block to my house. Even though she was slightly plump, she was in better shape than I was. She loved sports, while I spent a lot of time on my bottom watching her.

"I don't know. I guess they have to see if that's really me in the pictures. I suppose it's like when a company pulls out your résumé but wants you to come on a job interview anyway."

"Boy," Marilyn said, shaking her long hair out of her face, "I knew those long legs would come to some good someday—even if you are lousy at soccer."

"What do you mean lousy?" I protested. "I'm just afraid I'll hurt somebody. I could give you a good kick right now and show you."

"Never mind. But at least you should've given basketball a try."

"Who wants to run around throwing balls in nets? I've got better things to do with my time."

"Ah," Marilyn sighed. "It's such a waste."

"What are you talking about?" I poked her in the ribs. "I could never model with all those bruises on my body. . . . I know, you're just jealous, that's all."

"Jealous? Forget it. I hope I stay short and fat all my life."

I stopped dead in my tracks. According to our private rules, we were allowed to insult each other, but never ourselves. "You didn't say that, Marilyn," I said as we walked into the house.

"Sorry," she responded, grinning mischievously. "What I meant to say was, come on, let's wash your hair. It looks all stringy and greasy and gross."

"That's better." I smiled at my friend.

Once inside, I made a beeline for the shower and started on my hair. Anybody walking in would have seen one brunette in the shower and one blonde sitting cross-legged on the bathroom mat.

"I know why you're going to be a model," Marilyn proclaimed.

"Oh, yeah, smart mouth?"

"Uh-huh. You're doing it so you can be on that billboard that hangs over the baseball field and impress Greg."

I threw a bar of soap at her, but she ducked, and it hit the wall. "Ugh, I'd die if that happened. Besides, I don't have to impress him. He likes me already."

"I know. He asked me about you today."

"He *what*? What did he say? Why didn't you tell me?"

"He told me not to."

"If you don't tell me exactly what he told you right now," I warned, "you're in for a little surprise." I opened the shower curtain enough so that she could see I had the shower nozzle in my hand and was ready to aim it at her. "How are you at swimming?"

"Truce," she said, holding up her hands in front of her. "He just wanted to know if you were dating anybody else, that's all. I told him no. Next time he talks to me I'm going to ask him if his earlobe's been tingling this year."

"Marilyn, so help me, if you dare, I'll kill you!" I grabbed a towel, quickly wrapped it around me, then jumped out of the shower and chased her out of the bathroom and into the hall. But my hair was dripping all over the place, so I ran back in for another towel.

"Seriously, Marilyn, you've got to do me a

favor," I said as I rolled my hair into a towel. "Don't tell Greg about my modeling. I'd like him to hear about it from me. I have a feeling he's not going to be too thrilled with the idea."

"Why not? Wouldn't any guy be thrilled that his girlfriend's a model?"

"That's just it. Greg's not like most guys. He hates makeup and fashions."

"He sounds like a grind to me," Marilyn said doubtfully.

"Well, I think he's got the right idea. Why should a girl spend all her time on her looks just to please some dumb boy? I mean, there's more to me than my looks, and I for one am glad that Greg realizes that."

"Well, if you insist. . . ." Her voice trailed as she left the bathroom and went into my bedroom. I could hear her rummaging through my closet.

"I've got your outfit all picked out for you," she said when I walked into my bedroom a few minutes later. My skin glistened from the new body lotion I was trying out. Marilyn held up an oversized black sweater and tight stretch pants, along with my low ankle boots. "This way you can come back from the city and swing right into your date with Greg."

"Oh, I don't know, Marilyn," I said doubtfully. "That's a little wild, isn't it? Anyway,

Greg likes simpler things like flannel shirts and blue jeans. He's kind of an outdoors type."

"Oh, come on!" Marilyn's eyes sparkled. "Even a nature boy couldn't resist you in this. When you wore it to Pizzaz, you looked *stunning*!"

"Why, thanks, Marilyn," I replied dryly. "It isn't like you to compliment me."

"Everybody makes mistakes." Marilyn giggled. "What I meant was—you looked horrible, gross, and repulsive in it!"

"That's much better," I said. "Here, give me that. I'm freezing!"

When my mother came home a few moments later, I was dressed and halfway through drying my hair. I thought twenty minutes was pretty good time, myself, but it wasn't fast enough for Mom.

"Renée, what's going on in there?" she called from the hallway. Her voice sounded rushed.

"I'm drying my hair, Mom. Here. In my bedroom."

"You should be ready by now." Hearing her say that made me draw in my breath a little. Was it time already? I really had hurried as quickly as I could.

"My hair's so long," I called. "It's not quite

dry yet. But I'm all dressed and everything."

Suddenly Mom stood at the doorway, and I saw her look crossly at Marilyn, who was sitting on my bed reading magazines. "I told you there wasn't time for friends," she said. "How can I convey the message to you, Renée? This is *serious*."

"Marilyn helped me get dressed," I explained, casting my friend a look that meant: *I don't know what's with her but don't take it personally.*

Marilyn returned a glance that said: *Forget it. My mom gets grouchy, too.*

"You're not wearing that outfit," my mother stated flatly, looking disapprovingly at my clothes.

I stared back at her. "What's wrong with this? I wore it to Pizzaz a while ago, and everybody loved it."

"Oh, Pizzaz!" Mom sighed. "It looks like something you'd wear to a cheap little small-town disco. Put on a pair of tweed slacks and your red cable-knit sweater. The agency is looking for brunette preppy types now."

"Sure, Mom," I replied. I figured she would know, but I felt bad for Marilyn, who was only trying to help me. Besides, it really was my fault for not insisting that I come home alone. Luckily Marilyn knew just when to say good-bye and head for home. I found myself wondering what I would've done if Greg had come home with me instead.

Mom's mood changed as soon as I changed clothes. I could see her admiring me as I stood, looking preppy and classic. She paused in her own room just long enough to fetch an antique tortoise-shell headband. Then we put on our coats, jumped in the car, and were off.

Chapter Five

Entering the offices of the Photo Star modeling agency was like walking into the pages of an interior decorating magazine. The elevator opened to a slick little waiting room with ten stylish chrome chairs grouped around a futuristic-looking receptionist's desk. The girl at the desk looked young and beautiful, and I felt a bit uncomfortable as she looked me up and down with a critical eye. If Mom hadn't said, "Sit down while I tell the receptionist we're here," I would've been convinced she was the owner of the place. After my mother spoke to her, the receptionist stood, showed us a closet, where we hung up our coats, then walked into one of the offices off to the right. I was shocked to see that she was short, only about five feet, four inches in spite of her high, high heels. It occurred to me that she might have come here hoping to become a model but got the position as receptionist instead. No wonder, then, that she stared with contempt at every girl who walked in.

While we waited, several beautiful, tall, blonde models walked in. I recognized one immediately; her picture was on the cover of one of the teen fashion magazines I subscribed to.

"Mom!" I nudged my mother. "That was Lee Garrett—you know, from my last *Fashion Flair* magazine!"

Although she sat right next to me, Mom might as well have been two worlds away. She didn't answer me at all, but continued to stare at the door into which the receptionist had disappeared. The only movement she made was to pluck a thread off the sleeve of her suit. I guess inside she was feeling as nervous as I was.

Suddenly a woman appeared out of nowhere, smiling so wide it looked like it hurt. "Mrs. Renshaw?" she asked, coming forward and holding out her hand. "I'm Betty Floyde."

"I'm so pleased to meet you," my mother answered a little too quickly, rising to shake the glamorous-looking woman's hand. Then turning to me, she said, "This is Renée."

For a minute I sat speechless, not knowing what to do. Betty Floyde was well-known for having launched the careers of many of the top models in the business. I couldn't believe I was going to be dealing directly with her. Still, I was uncertain. Should I also rise and shake hands with Mrs. Floyde? Or should I just smile and say, "Hello, it's nice to meet you"?

Before I could say anything, the Photo Star director glanced at her watch and said, "I've already made an appointment for us this afternoon. The *Miss* magazine people are staying late just to see Renée, so we've got to hurry. It's very important."

With that she turned and beckoned us to follow. Mom nearly tripped over her feet in her enthusiasm to keep up, and looking down, I noticed she was wearing a new pair of high-heeled shoes I'd never seen before.

I wondered what Betty Floyde meant about *Miss* magazine. Why did the people who put out one of the very magazines I subscribed to want to meet me? Did they want me to model for them? The thought made me shiver with excitement. That would be too much to believe.

Betty Floyde motioned us into a very large office, and we sat down while she excused herself and ran out again. It seemed hard for this woman to sit still, if at all. So far I'd only seen her run.

While Mom and I waited for her return, I looked around at the walls. They were papered from top to bottom with photographs of beautiful young women, one more gorgeous than the next. Most were framed pictures of magazine covers, but here and there were also a couple of eight-by-ten-inch black and white photographs. Probably the newer models, I thought. One of them caught my eye, and I had the strangest sensation.

"Mom!" I nudged my mother again, barely concealing a gasp. "Look over there—that's me!"

"I told you," my mother said proudly. "The pictures were so good they took you right away. Pretty soon you'll be on one of those covers over there."

"But I can't believe it can happen so fast," I said, practically squealing. "Don't I have to go to a modeling school first or something?"

"No," I heard someone answer. Mrs. Floyde had returned, with two girls trailing behind her. One was plump, with curly, short red hair and lots of blue eyeshadow; the other was blonde and wore no makeup at all. "To answer your question," the agency director continued, "we don't believe in modeling schools here. We like our models to respond naturally to the camera, not in some practiced, contrived way. Renée, these are your bookers, Gail and Lucinda. They'll be charting your appointments, taking your bookings, helping you get around, and so on."

"Hi," I said meekly. Although these girls couldn't have been much older than I, they looked as sophisticated as the models on the magazine covers.

"Hi," they answered in unison. Lucinda, the blonde, looked friendly and cheerful, but Gail seemed cold. She looked me up and down critically the way the receptionist had, and I found I had to look away from her direct stare.

"Gail," Mrs. Floyde ordered. "Take Renée's measurements, please, while I call *Miss* magazine and tell them we're on our way."

Then while I stood, Gail pulled out a measuring tape and proceeded to measure every single part of my body. Mom had measured me once around the bust, waist, and hips for some clothes she was ordering from a catalog, but I felt embarrassed about having a complete stranger do it. I glanced over to my mother for sympathy, but she wasn't even looking my way. Mrs. Floyde had handed her a contract to sign, and she was busy reading the fine print.

Lucinda, meanwhile, sat on the corner of the director's desk and filled out a large white chart. "Hair: dark brown? Eyes: light brown?"

She called out the entries, questioning each one so anybody who wanted to could disagree.

"Hazel," Mrs. Floyde corrected from where she sat conferring with my mother.

"They look like plain old brown to me," Gail snorted as she continued to measure me. She obviously didn't think much of me. The feeling was growing more mutual by the minute.

"Say hazel," Mrs. Floyde said. "It sounds better. Anyway, they're light brown, so they can be easily color corrected in a photograph if need be. Unfortunately, it is better to have light eyes in this business."

What's wrong with brown eyes? I wondered, and then I noticed Mom glance over at me nervously. Only she didn't really look at *me*, she looked at my eyes. I could guess what she was thinking: "If only she had my blue eyes instead of Dad's." For a second, I felt confused. All my life Mom had loved my brown eyes. Did she want me to have blue eyes now instead, just because of what the director of this agency had said?

"Height: five feet, eight inches?" Lucinda continued.

"Weight: a hundred ten?" She looked at me doubtfully.

"She looks much heavier," Gail said. "But we don't have time to get the scale out today. Don't gain any more weight," she told me.

44

"Bust: thirty-two A?" Lucinda said. Mrs. Floyde looked up from the contract she and my mother were signing. "It's too bad you're not a little bigger in the bust. There's a lot of swimsuit work right now."

"She's still developing," my mother put in quickly. "I'm sure she'll be a thirty-four B in a year or two."

As thrilled as I was with the prospect of going to *Miss* magazine, I was beginning to feel uncomfortable about the way I was being treated. How could these people—even my own mother—talk about me like I wasn't even there? I didn't even feel like a real person.

Finally Lucinda and Gail finished the chart, and Mrs. Floyde reached for her coat. "Now that the details are behind us," she said, "let's run to *Miss* magazine. It's getting late."

Before I could say, "Wait, what's going on here?" I was handed my coat by my mother and hastened out of the office and into the elevator. Down in the street, Mrs. Floyde flagged down a cab.

"Renée's a special girl." Mrs. Floyde smiled at my mother after we'd all sat down in the back seat of the taxi. I didn't know whether my mother or I was supposed to say thank you. Not once had Mrs. Floyde spoken to me. I felt as if I were nothing more than a walking mannequin being readied for display. I didn't like it. Is this what being a model was about?

"Thank you, I always thought so myself." I was relieved to hear Mom speak. She smiled at me, but it still felt funny, as if I didn't have anything to do with any of it.

"I'm sure the editors at *Miss* will think so," Mrs. Floyde went on. "They're desperate for a brunette, and they simply went wild over Renée's photographs. And that's saying a lot, considering the photographer wasn't even very good."

"Wouldn't *Miss* rather use a more experienced model?" I asked. From the corner of my eye I could see Mom glaring at me.

"Oh, just the opposite!" Mrs. Floyde chuckled. "The magazines are always looking for new discoveries. If the model's even been around for a month, they start losing interest. So it's up to me to send them everything new that comes along."

The thought of being part of "everything new that comes along" felt strange. Marilyn would get a kick out of hearing it, though.

The taxi zigzagged in and out of traffic, and before long we arrived at the *Miss* editorial offices. We went up in an elevator to the twentieth floor, where the receptionist took our coats, then directed us straight to a pair of closed double doors that led to some sort of conference room. Before we went in, Mrs. Floyde stopped to straighten my collar and pull lint off my sweater. Mom got a brush out of her pocketbook and smoothed my hair. I could feel the tension they felt rise up in my body. If *Miss* magazine didn't like me, all this would be for nothing. What if I messed up and spoiled everything?

I was about to lean over to Mom and whisper, "What should I say?" but it was too late. Mrs. Floyde opened the double doors, and there, seated around a huge table the length of a drawing room, were the editors of *Miss*. I counted thirteen heads as I walked in on faltering legs, and I could feel the stare of all twenty-six eyes penetrate like X rays straight through my body.

Mrs. Floyde put her arm around my shoulders and held me affectionately, as if we'd known each other for years. "Ladies, this is Renée," she said. "Isn't she a beauty?"

I expected some sort of response just then. Maybe they would say hello, or maybe they'd say "She's ugly—throw her out!" Instead, a very strange thing happened. A low murmur, which started as a slight hum and then grew to a roar, very nearly filled the gigantic room. The ladies were all bent over the table, talking among themselves, and seeming to ignore us completely. When I first watched them, I was puzzled, but then when I saw them look and stare at me, I understood: *they were talking about me*!

"This is an emergency editorial meeting," Mrs. Floyde explained, whispering to Mom and me. "They've decided not to go with the cover they had shot for the next issue, and they're desperately looking for a new model."

I heard her words, but they didn't quite sink in. I was watching a meeting, that was all, and some girl was going to be chosen to do the May cover. It was impossible to really comprehend it might be me. However, Mom looked flushed and nervous when I looked over at her, and I knew that was exactly what they were considering at this very moment. I began to feel more nervous than ever.

Finally the woman at the head of the table spoke. She seemed old, but her gray hair was cut in a youngish page-boy style, and she almost dripped with belts, scarves, and bracelets.

"We want to shoot Renée right now," she said to Mrs. Floyde. "Can she stay?"

"Yes," my mother answered immediately.

"Fine," the senior editor agreed before I had a chance to speak. "The *Miss* studio is on the twenty-first floor, and I'll be up to meet you there in a few minutes. Why don't you go up there now so the makeup artist can start on Renée? The photographer is Hans Von Hammel. He's quite well known, and I'm sure you'll like him."

"Go ahead," Mrs. Floyde told my mother quietly. "I have to stay here for a while longer and discuss the modeling fees with the editors. You understand," she went on, looking at me but speaking to Mom, "that *Miss* does not pay the regular advertising fees to models. As for editorial, they pay considerably less. However, the widespread publicity Renée will receive for posing on the cover will lead to countless other bookings."

"I understand." Mom nodded, and then she and I left and retraced our steps to the elevator. Once inside, I pressed the button for the twenty-first floor and turned to her.

"I've got to make a phone call," I told her.

"Why?" she said. "You can tell your friends all about this tomorrow."

"That's not why," I explained. "I have to cancel my date with Greg."

"Oh, all right, go ahead and call," Mom said when the elevator stopped and let us off. "Go ask the receptionist for the phone. I'll be waiting right here. Get it over with before the makeup artist starts on you."

When I first heard Greg's voice saying hello, I got temporary lockjaw. My teeth felt as if they were glued together.

"Hello," I managed to say feebly. "This is Renée."

"Renée!" Greg exclaimed. "What's up?" He sounded glad to hear from me, and that made me feel even more miserable. If things had worked out the way they were supposed to, I would've been seeing him soon. "Have you been working on your essay?" he continued. "I took a glance at mine again, and, boy, it really needs help!"

"I've been real busy, too, Greg," I replied. "In fact, I'm calling to . . . to tell you I can't see you tonight. I—I'm sorry, but it's an emergency."

Greg's voice sounded so wonderfully concerned, I could've melted right on the spot. "I'm sorry to hear that. Is there anything I can do to help?"

"Oh no, it's nothing like that. You see— uh—my mother took me into New York with her. It's about a job," I said, stretching the truth a little. I thought it best to explain everything to Greg in person.

"You don't have to explain, Renée," Greg said softly. Although he was all the way over in Eastbrooke, he might as well have been standing right next to me by the way it felt. "I understand."

"You do?" I asked, disbelieving.

"Hey, do I look some kind of hard-hearted ogre?" He chuckled and then added, "Of course you should be with your mother. She needs you. So don't worry about tonight," he continued. "I'll still see you tomorrow, right? And Renée?"

"Yes?"

"Tell your mom good luck for me."

Suddenly Mom's head appeared from behind the booth.

"Honey!" she said, "Hurry up! We haven't got much time. The editors are waiting for us in the studio."

Reluctantly I said goodbye to Greg and hung up the phone. Then I followed my anxiety-ridden mother to the studio. She turned to me and nervously tilted my chin up high with her finger. I had to be courageous; I was going to be a star.

Chapter Six

I'd never realized how much hard work went into modeling before I posed for the *Miss* cover. It took them nearly three hours from the time I first stood before the camera before they felt they had enough photos to work with. Even so, they told me there was a possibility of calling me back for more shooting. First, they took pictures of me wearing shorts and a matching shirt. In these shots my hair was hanging down, the way I usually wear it, only they brought in a fan to make my hair fly. Then they sent me back to the dressing room, where the makeup lady changed my makeup, put my hair into a ponytail, and had me change into a jogging outfit.

Even though posing before the camera was tiring, Hans Von Hammel, the photographer, made the work feel easy. He kept up a running conversation with me, putting in a few jokes here and there to make me laugh. I could feel myself gradually losing my self-consciousness, and by the end of the session, I was as relaxed as if I were hanging out with Marilyn in my bedroom. This is a lot of fun, I told myself as I was changing back into my real clothes. When I was in front of the camera, I felt as if I was living out a fantasy.

It was close to eight o'clock by the time we left the *Miss* offices. Mom kept repeating how thrilled the editors were with their selection of me and how they liked the natural way I acted in front of the camera. Late in the session, one of the editors had approached Mom and told her she had a new star on her hands. It was such a wild concept that it was still hard to believe it was really happening to me.

It would have been perfect—if I hadn't told Greg that little white lie. Walking along the cold, dark city street in search of a taxi, I felt guilty about not being totally honest with him. Yet something told me he wouldn't be pleased to hear the truth, especially since it meant we wouldn't be able to see each other as often as we'd like. Come to think of it, *I* didn't like that much, either. The thought made me shiver.

"Not cold, are you, honey?" My mother looked at me anxiously. She'd always fretted over me like an overprotective mother hen, but until today it had never really bothered me. Already, however, I could see that from now on she'd cluck whenever I sneezed or felt tired or had a headache or a pimple or anything that might jeopardize my modeling career.

"I'm okay," I answered, looking away from her.

She hailed a cab, and we got in. Suddenly I felt exhausted. I leaned back against the seat of the cab and stared out the window. I didn't feel like talking.

As we came to the lot where our car was parked, my mother said, "I can see that missed night's sleep is finally catching up with you. You always tend to get depressed when you're tired. I guess I can't blame you if you are now. You've certainly had some day!" She counted on her fingers. "First, you stayed up all night, then you ran home from school, traveled to New York, were accepted by the top agency in town, and now you've been photographed for the cover of the top teen magazine in the country. For anybody else, that would be enough for a lifetime!"

The taxi had stopped by the parking lot, and as my mother paid the driver, I noticed that her jaw was set and her face was flushed, much like the people I saw running past us from all directions. There was something in the air in New York City that charged people up. I didn't know exactly what it was, but I could feel it, too, in the slight chill that kept traveling up my spine and into my skull. It made people race and compete with each other and run after dreams or money or fame. My mother was stung with it, too. I could tell from the way she talked on and on while we waited for the attendant to get our car. Her voice was high-pitched, and she talked at me instead of to me, not listening to what I said.

"We'll take a monthly pass for the car," Mom told the parking lot attendant when we reached the exit booth. I saw her hand the guy five twenty-dollar bills.

"One hundred dollars for parking!" I gasped when we pulled out of the lot into the street.

"That's how much it costs to park in New York," Mom replied. "We could take the train in, but there aren't many that run late in the afternoon. Besides, we'll probably be carrying a lot of things, like clothes, model bags, portfolios, and so on."

"But one hundred dollars is half your salary," I protested. "We can't afford it, can we?"

I thought I saw my mother wince when I said that.

"Not to worry," she told me. "To make money you have to spend money."

It was another one of those sayings that Mrs. Milton would have labeled cliché. But it was true of my mother. And it was a side of her I'd never seen. She didn't mind sacrificing half her paycheck if it meant I might make money. Just then, she turned from the steering wheel and flashed me an odd little smile, which made me feel funny all over. It seemed almost as if *she* were embarking on my modeling career, not me.

A half hour later we had made our way through the heavy outgoing city traffic. When we exited the Lincoln Tunnel and entered the dusk beyond, I felt as if we'd just been regurgitated out of a long, grimy snake. The image pleased me, and I thought of starting a new story about New York for the writing contest. But thinking of it made me sit up straight in my seat. When would I have time to write the essay?

"Honey, try to relax," Mom said just then. I must have been doing a lot of fidgeting, thinking about Greg and the writing contest and the way my life would be changing.

"I was just thinking about school—" I began.

"Oh, Renée." My mother sighed. "Don't worry, you'll do fine. You're an excellent student as it is, and if your grades went down a bit, it wouldn't make any difference to me."

"It wouldn't?" I said, surprised. "Anyway, it's not just school. I'm just wondering how I'm going to juggle all my other activities with the modeling."

"You may have to give up some of them," Mom said understandingly. "I know it's a lot to ask from you, but in order to achieve success you have to make some sacrifices."

Another dumb saying, I thought. I'd just make time for Greg, if nothing else—there was no way I was going to give *him* up!

"That reminds me," Mom went on. "I meant to have a talk with you, and right now is as good a time as any."

"What is it, Mom?" I looked over at her, but I saw only the faint outline of her profile.

"It's what I was saying to you this morning about getting enough sleep. It's a good thing you're young and your skin springs right back into shape after a couple of hours—I should be so lucky myself. But if you make a practice of staying up late, your bad habits will catch up with you, and you'll start looking awful. You can't afford that now."

"Yes, Mom . . . "

"And you'll have a very busy schedule from now on. Besides the calls, you'll be expected to go to meetings at the agency, beauty seminars, cocktail parties—"

"Cocktail parties?" I echoed. The only party I expected to go to was the April Fool's party in school next month. The one I hoped to go to with Greg.

"Yes, cocktail parties," Mom repeated. "If you're going to be a successful model, it's very important for you to get around and meet people. There must be thousands of photographers and art directors in the city, and the only way you can possibly meet them is at those parties. But don't get your hopes up—I wouldn't consider letting you go without me!"

"Will there be celebrities there?" I asked.

"Perhaps—and that's another thing, Renée. You can't afford to be so wide-eyed about everything. You're a professional now, and this is a very competitive business. There's no room in it for starry-eyed innocence."

"Okay, Mom, I'll try. But it'll be pretty hard to be calm when I shake hands with someone famous."

"I know," she said, smiling.

Mom pulled the old Ford off the highway onto the road leading into Eastbrooke. "You're happy, aren't you?" she asked hopefully.

"Sure, Mom, why wouldn't I be?"

She sighed. "I just hope I'm doing the right

thing. You have a God-given talent, and I think it's my duty as your mother to see that you take advantage of that talent while you can."

"Mom, I suppose I should have asked you this before, but there's something I still don't understand. What made you do this?"

She took my hand just then, and from the slight rasp in her voice, I could tell she was about to tell me something important. "When you were born, Renée, your father and I wanted only the best for you. We moved out here to Eastbrooke thinking it would be a good place for you to grow up, to play, to meet lots of friends. When your father died, it put a big burden on me. I had to go to work to support us, and the only job I could get paid enough to cover only the bare essentials. I hoped that in time I'd be able to work myself up to a higher position, but that hasn't happened. Ever since you started high school, I've been worrying about how I was going to send you to college. Sure, there's your father's trust fund, but with costs today that'll barely get you through one year."

"I didn't know that," I said.

"Well, I guess that's my fault. I didn't want you to worry. Anyway," she went on, "one day I turned around and saw how you'd turned into a beautiful young lady. I thought back to when you were seven and I had made the rounds of the modeling agencies with you. A few of the agencies then thought you had potential and told me to try again when you got older. I thought it was worth it to give it another shot, and my hunch paid off. Do you realize how much you'll be making? One hundred dollars an hour. In one year you can make enough by modeling to pay for your education at any college in the country. We'd be fools to walk away from an opportunity like that."

"One hundred dollars an hour!" I gasped.

She nodded, then turned her attention back to the wheel and guided the car onto Main Street in Eastbrooke.

Another thought struck me, and I voiced it out loud. "But if I'm successful and make a lot of money, won't it bother you that I'm paid more than you are for a lot less work?"

"No," she said, grinning oddly. "As it happens, I plan to quit my job and become your brand-new personal manager!"

And with that, the car swung into our street and up the driveway to the white clapboard cottage we called home.

Chapter Seven

On Saturday morning I woke up early after dreaming all night about Greg. I knew I'd been dreaming about him because I felt a longing deep down inside of me when I opened my eyes to the sun streaming into the windows. I couldn't wait until nine o'clock when I'd see him again.

I sat up on the bed with a jolt. I'd never had a chance to tell Mom I'd be spending all day with Greg. When we had arrived home from Manhattan, I'd gone straight to my room, to bed. Now I didn't dare wake her up—Saturday was her day to sleep late.

Nevertheless, she would've been proud of how quickly I got ready that morning. By 8:15 I'd finished my shower, and five minutes later I was dressed. My hair took a bit longer to dry, but since I didn't bother styling it or putting on makeup, I was ready and waiting outside the door when Greg and his friends came at 8:45.

"You didn't have to bring anything." Greg grinned when he saw the picnic basket I was carrying. "We have enough for an army as it is."

"It's nothing much," I said. "Just some fruit and stuff."

I didn't bother to add that the "fruit and stuff" meant diet foods. Before I'd gone to sleep, Mom had told me that the agency had suggested I could lose a pound or two. I had decided I might as well get started right away on losing it, so I hadn't packed anything fattening.

"Whew!" Greg commented when he lifted the basket into the trunk of the car. "It's 'nothing much,' is it? I'll bet it's a twenty-pound chocolate cake!"

"Oh, no!" I gasped, laughing. That got the attention of Greg's cousins, Tom and Chris, who hung out of the window of the car to grin at me. Tom was dark-haired and brown-eyed and looked to me to be the older of the two. Chris was blond, and I could spot a family resemblance to Greg in his twinkling blue eyes and freckled nose.

"Sh-h-h-h, you'll wake my mother," I warned, holding a finger in front of my lips.

"I'm supposed to be home today doing all kinds of chores and things."

For a minute I imagined everybody would look at me like I was some kind of Mama's girl, but nobody did. Instead, they smiled and quietly let themselves be introduced by Greg. Tom's girlfriend Mary was about my age and wore her long blonde hair in a big French braid. Judy, Chris's girlfriend, had short dark hair and sparkling green eyes. She sat next to me in the back, with Chris up front with Tom and Mary so that Greg and I could sit together. Everybody seemed to be very sweet and accommodating, and I was happy. I had always hoped Greg's friends would be like that, if I ever met them—and they were.

"Did you really sneak out on your mother?" Greg asked after Tom turned the car out of my street and everybody had settled down.

"It's okay," I said. "I left a note. Anyway, Mom doesn't get up until about noon on Saturdays. She loves to sleep late. She's what you call a 'night person.' It really kills her to get up early during the week and go to work!"

As Greg chuckled near my ear, I could feel his breath brush the side of my freshly washed hair. The warmth felt good, and for a moment I couldn't believe I was really sitting next to him. It was such a contrast to being with the people in the modeling agency or the editors of *Miss* magazine or Hans Von Hammel. Those were all well-known people I'd never in a million years have expected to meet or talk to. That was exciting, sure, but being with Greg was exciting, too, in a different kind of way. Unlike some famous person, he was somebody I always expected I'd be with someday, and feeling his body against mine whenever we drove over bumps in the road or took sharp turns to the left or right filled me with anticipation for the day ahead. Deep down inside I knew Mom wouldn't be too happy when she read the note, but I figured she'd understand.

"Yeah, I know what that means!" Tom agreed from the front. "I'm a night person, too, and look at me now. If it wasn't for Mary here and my dumb cousins, who all want to go hiking, I'd be all warm and toasty in bed right now."

"You poor sick old man!" Mary poked him in the ribs, and Chris and Judy joined in the laughter.

"How about you?" I heard Greg whisper in my ear. "Are you a night or day person?"

For a second my impulse was to find out what Greg was first and then go along with him. But then I realized that wouldn't make any difference. He liked me for who I was.

"Day," I stated confidently. "Especially morning. I just love it when the sun shines through my windows at the crack of dawn. I feel like the whole world's asleep except for me, the sun, and the birds."

I don't know why I gave away all this so easily. For a minute afterward everybody was quiet. I thought Greg or the others might laugh at what I said or think I was weird or something. I held my breath, waiting for their reaction.

Then I looked up at Greg's face. I saw that he was smiling gently at me, as if he understood every single thing I'd said and agreed with it wholeheartedly. Then I felt his lips next to my ear once more. "Me, too," he said softly and happily. It was as if we had just agreed on something far more important than what time of day we loved best.

The rest of the day was probably one of the happiest in my whole life. After we arrived at Bear Lake State Forest twenty minutes later, we all tumbled out of the car and put the food in little day packs that Tom and Chris kept in the trunk of the car. Then, looking like Snow White's seven dwarfs minus one, we started our hike up Beaver Trail.

It was six miles to the summit, but with

Greg helping me climb and with everyone laughing and talking, it seemed like a very short hike.

I liked Tom, Mary, Chris, and Judy; they were so much like Greg and me. We all seemed to love the same things—things that I know a lot of kids in school would've considered stupid. As we hiked, we played a game in which we tried to name as many plants around us as we could. I was miserable at it, but I tried to hide my ignorance by making up names as I went along. No one believed me, but Greg did give me points for originality.

At one point Chris broke off a large, red-veined leaf from a forest plant and swished it under our noses.

"Ugh!" exclaimed Judy. "It stinks."

"Like skunk!" Tom described it.

"Well, what do you expect?" Greg put in. "It's called skunk cabbage."

"Do skunks eat it for breakfast?" Judy asked, her eyes twinkling and looking greener than ever. She was spunky, and I liked her.

"Of course not!" Tom scoffed at her.

"Well—why not?" she persisted. "After all, you are what you eat!"

The conversation got so ridiculous we all burst out laughing. Minutes later we reached the top of the mountain. It was bare, like an old man's bald head, and we spread a blanket out on the dry grass. In full view below us was the clear expanse of Bear Lake, which Greg told me got its name from its unusual shape. Although the trees were still bare and the landscape looked bleak, the temperature was in the upper fifties. We felt as if we were the only people to ever experience this place, and it was a great feeling to have.

We unpacked the food, then sat on the blanket and ate lunch. The others had brought sandwiches, so they appreciated the fruits and vegetables I had brought along.

After the meal, Tom lay back in the grass holding a long brown reed in his mouth. Mary snuggled up next to him. Chris and Judy leaned back against a tree stump, staring at the clear view of rolling hills. Only Greg and I were still eating lunch, and for a second I felt awkward. The others had been couples for a while already, but Greg and I had only been together for two days. Up to now, it had been easy sitting next to him in the car, hiking in a group, and talking to the others. But now the rest of them were pairing off, and Greg and I looked at each other a bit nervously.

I looked away for a while, pretending to study the horizon. I could feel Greg looking at me, but something kept me from looking back. Then suddenly he spoke. "Want to go for a walk? You can see the New York skyline from the other side of this mountain."

"Sure," I agreed. It seemed like a pretty good idea to get away from the others. Tom and Mary were beginning to kiss a little, and I was a little embarrassed seeing them while Greg was sitting next to me. In a way I wished Greg and I had been together long enough to do that, too; but I was just as glad to take things slowly. I wanted our relationship to last a long time.

"How long have Tom and Mary been together?" I asked after we'd walked out of earshot of the others.

"Since their sophomore year," Greg said. "Now they're freshmen in college. Tom's like an older brother to me, and Mary's been around since I was a kid in eighth grade. I guess you could say they're like an old married couple."

"Oh, I see," I said, but I didn't. Did Greg mean it was good or bad to be like an "old married couple?" I hoped he meant good.

The top of the mountain was tiny compared to its base, and in a matter of minutes we'd reached the other side. What I saw there made me hold my breath: there, in the hazy distance, was the New York City skyline. The tall, gray buildings rose up from the horizon like stone monuments to another time. I couldn't believe that I'd worked in that place just yesterday. It seemed so far away, so unreal, so removed from the peaceful grassy mountaintop where Greg and I now stood. For a moment we watched together, feeling each other's presence, but not saying a word.

"Remember our conversation before about day people and night people?" Greg asked as he stood gazing at the fantastic skyline.

"Yes?" I said. A cloud moved in the distance, and for a minute, only the tops of the buildings were visible. For a second I wished they would disappear altogether, as if they didn't exist at all. Then I could stay here with Greg forever.

"Well," Greg continued dreamily, shading his eyes with his hand and looking ahead of him, "sometimes I come here alone real early, like on a Sunday morning, and I'll stand here and think: I'm awake, and there are eight million people down there who are asleep. That's when I know I'm really a day person. I feel like I'm the only person in the whole world. It's a great feeling!"

"I feel like that, too," I put in. In a way, Greg was telling me he felt alone, and I wanted to let him know it didn't have to be that way. All those early Sunday mornings I had been right down below in the valley, lying awake in my bed in a little white clapboard house in East-brooke and thinking of him.

"Do you, Renée?" Greg looked at me.

"Yes, I really do."

"Maybe you'd like to come up here with me tomorrow, then. Spring is just beginning, and there are so many things I could show you that we didn't see today. Like the first wood daisies, for instance, and birds' nests." His face lit up. "And did you ever see a real live fawn?"

From the way my heart was racing at that moment, you'd think we'd just finished climbing Mount Everest instead of Bear Lake Mountain. I was so excited that I could hardly even manage to catch my breath.

"Yes!" I gasped, as if my life depended on it. I added, "I'd love to come here with you again. I love the outdoors more than anything in the world."

"I knew that," Greg said. "I knew you were an outdoors kind of girl by the things you always say in English class. Remember our discussion on Thoreau?"

I nodded but couldn't say a thing. I was speechless with happiness.

"You know you look so pretty today," he said, touching his finger to my cheek. "The hike's made your cheeks rosy, and your eyes shine. Just like a nature girl."

"Thanks, Greg," I whispered.

"And you thought you needed all that makeup to get me to like you. Now wasn't that silly?"

"Yes," was all I could say.

"You know," he went on, "I think about all the money my kid sister Jane spends on makeup and those stupid fashion magazines, and it just makes me sick. All the effort made to teach girls how to be deceptive and pretend to be something they're not. You know what I mean?"

Do I ever, I thought dully. The funny thing was I really did agree with some of what he was saying. I agreed it was silly to go out and spend a lot of money on an outfit that I saw in a magazine, only to be told a few months later that it was out of style. On the other hand, I couldn't deny how thrilled I was with the prospect of having my picture on the cover of the biggest, most important teenage magazine in the country. Realizing that I was being a little bit of a hypocrite only made me feel worse. Now how could I tell Greg the truth about what I had done on Friday? He'd see how hypocritical I was and definitely never want to see me again!

Greg misunderstood my silence. "Oh, there I go, boring you again." He came over and put his arms around me. A breeze came up and blew my hair around, and he pulled me closer to him. "Let's talk about something else. Look, there's your house," he said, pointing to the west. "You can only see a white spot from here, but I know it's yours because there's the bank building on the next block."

I strained my eyes to look. "But you can hardly see anything," I protested. "It's only a faint white speck in the distance. You have to guess it's my house at all."

"I use my imagination." Greg grinned. "Just like I used to imagine going out with you."

I looked up at him. "You used to daydream about going out with *me*?" I couldn't believe we had both been doing the same thing.

He nodded. "I noticed you the first day you walked into English class."

Greg's hair was all tossed and windblown now by the mountain breeze that enveloped us from all sides. In his flannel shirt, his worn-out jeans, and leather vest, he looked like some lone woodsman from out West somewhere. It was hard to imagine him sitting cramped into a desk in English class at school. Yet he was a good student, too, and had the gentle sensitivity that also made him an excellent writer. He was everything I'd ever wanted in a boy. I hoped with all my heart that I was everything he'd waited for, too. But I couldn't tell him about the modeling. Maybe one day, when he loved me too much for it to matter, I would tell him, but not yet.

"Greg?" I said suddenly.

"Mmm?" he replied. "What?"

"Nothing," I said. "I just want to make sure it's really you holding me this minute."

"It is," he murmured into my ear. "Is it really you I'm holding?"

And then we kissed each other for a long, long time.

A while later we walked arm in arm to the other side of the mountain where the others were waiting. When we got there, they had already packed our gear into the little day packs. Even the litter was neatly put away.

"What kept you two?" Chris asked us when we returned. His tone was insinuatingly teasing, and the others all looked at us curiously.

"Oh, nothing much." Greg smiled, hugging me closer to him. "We just went over to the other side to have a look at the New York skyline." Then he added, looking at me with a twinkle in his eye, "It's something I've always wanted to show my girl."

Chapter Eight

That night Marilyn called me late, after I'd already gone to bed and fallen asleep. But that didn't stop me from getting the phone when it rang. I always thought that even if I didn't wake up, I'd still sleepwalk to the phone.

"How was your date with Greg?" She giggled. I figured she'd just come back from a crazy night at Pizzaz.

"Sh-h-h," I told her. "You'll wake my mother."

"You're nuts! How can she hear me over the phone? You're the one who has to speak softly."

"Oh, yeah. I forgot. I'm not too bright when I'm half asleep."

"So I noticed." Marilyn laughed. "Now what about Greg?"

"He's great," I said, brightening.

"So what did you do?"

"We hiked to the top of Bear Lake Mountain with his friends. Marilyn, it was the most wonderful day in my life."

"I knew you two would hit it off," she said. "By the way, how'd it go at the agency yesterday? You rat. You never called."

"I didn't get back till late. I had to stay in town to pose for the cover of *Miss* magazine." I emphasized the last two words and waited for Marilyn's reaction.

For a second there was complete silence. Then Marilyn nearly blasted my ear off. "Renée!" she squealed. "You made it! Great! I knew you would."

I then gave her a blow-by-blow account of the entire day.

"My friend, the model," Marilyn said proudly. "Wait till the kids in school hear about it!"

"Wait, Marilyn," I pleaded. "Do me a big favor."

"Sure, anything for the star."

"Don't tell anybody yet."

"What?"

"You heard me. I want this to be between us two only."

"Us? Didn't you tell Greg?"

"Marilyn!" I yelled. "That's just the point! I tried to tell him, but I couldn't."

"I don't get it."

"Like I told you the other day—he thinks I'm some kind of outdoors person—you know, a real nature type."

"So? You are."

"I know. But he'll never believe it now if he knows I'm a model. He made a big point of telling me how much he hates makeup and all that stuff."

"I don't believe it," Marilyn grumbled. "How are you going to explain why you can't see him on weekdays?"

"I told him I had to go into town with Mom on business. I kinda gave him the impression I'm helping her find a new job."

"What about when he sees the issue of *Miss* with you on the cover?" Marilyn persisted. "What're you going to do then?"

"It won't be out for another month. By then things will be different," I insisted.

"Okay," Marilyn agreed. "I won't tell a soul. But you're really asking a lot of me. Now I finally know somebody famous, and I can't even talk about it!"

"How was Pizzaz tonight?" I asked, trying to change the subject.

"Great. The band was really tight. I thought I'd see you there in that black outfit your mother hates so much."

"Nah, I couldn't get over there."

"Why? Greg?"

"No, my mom. She was furious when I got home after my date with him."

"You're kidding!"

"No. With everything that's gone on around here, I never got a chance to tell her about our date. I left before she'd even gotten up, and I found out later that she'd expected me to spend the day with her."

"What for?"

"She wanted me to go and buy modeling supplies with her. You know, like makeup, underwear, stockings, combs, brushes—the whole works. Then tonight I had to sit down with her and learn makeup tricks. She even made me do exercises."

"Ugh!" Marilyn groaned. "What a bore. Didn't you tell her you had just hiked up that whole mountain?"

"We made a deal. I spent tonight with her so I could spend tomorrow morning with Greg."

"Another date?"

"Yeah, but I have to be back by noon. Homework," I grumbled.

"Being a star does have its price."

"Tell me about it," I groaned. "I'll see you Monday."

"I'll be looking for glitter," Marilyn said cheerfully.

Chapter Nine

Trying to juggle school, modeling, and Greg became a nearly impossible task, but I wouldn't quite admit that to myself. Instead, I tried to separate the three worlds into totally different lives and live them all at the same time. Between the time I got up at 6:30 A.M. until 2:30 P.M. I was Renée, the student. I tried to listen extra carefully and take detailed notes in every class because I knew there wouldn't be much time to study when exam time came around. I crammed homework into my one study period as best I could, and I even did it during lunch break.

But I ran into problems.

"You're no fun anymore since you decided to be Miss Perfect," Marilyn complained one day over her cottage cheese.

"I can't help it," I protested. "I've got all this work and no time to do it."

"You have time to hike up that stupid

mountain with Greg every Sunday morning," she taunted.

"Oh, Marilyn. You're not even up yet at that time of the morning. Anyway, do you expect me to give him up or something? You're just crabby because you're on one of your stupid diets again."

But my best friend seemed to have outgrown our mutual insult society. To my amazement she actually got up to join Julie and some of the other girls at the other end of the table. I felt hurt for a moment, but then I went back to my homework. I had no time to fret. Some things were more important than others, and Marilyn would just have to understand. There'd be time for her later.

The other person who gave me trouble in school was Mrs. Milton. Every day after class she would give me a long questioning look that meant, "How are you coming along on your essay?" I didn't have the heart to tell her I wasn't coming along at all on it. Instead, I found myself gradually resenting her. Didn't she know I spent study periods and Sunday nights doing the regular English homework? Didn't she know I was helping Greg with his essay? The last thing I had time for was that stupid essay for the contest. It had laid discarded on my desk for weeks, a casualty of this whole modeling thing. I knew I'd never finish it in time, but somehow I felt I had to keep Mrs. Milton believing I would. I guess I didn't want to lose out at being one of her best students.

And then at 2:30 sharp I became Renée, the model. Mom would be waiting in the old Ford in the front parking lot, and as soon as I got in, we would zoom off to New York. My first appointments were always scheduled for 3:30, and in a business where the competition was fierce, I couldn't afford to be late even once.

Although getting into the agency and landing my first cover for *Miss* had seemed so easy, Mom warned me the hard part would come later. "You were just lucky," she made a point of telling me over and over again. "You were at the right place at the right time. People are fickle in this business—they're always looking for new faces. The real trick isn't getting in—it's staying in."

Still, landing that *Miss* cover did seem to open some doors. They called me back for an eye makeup layout the following week. Despite Mrs. Floyde's worry, they loved my brown eyes. The makeup artist, Sara, was a doll and made that shoot lots of fun for me. A former model herself, she regaled me with lots of gossip about many of the other models, along with inside information about the business.

In fact, Sara's recommendation got me my

next job, modeling makeup for a department store catalog. That job was done at a much faster pace than the jobs for *Miss*—but it paid a lot more, too. It was also my first job working with other models, two blondes who'd been modeling for several years each. I'd have expected them to look down on me because I was new, but they were really very friendly, sharing some of their beauty tips with me and wishing me good luck.

Most of my time was spent going from place to place on "go-sees" where I would "go see" prospective clients who might want to use me somewhere down the line!

One day on my way into the city I tried doing some of my homework in the car. Mom made me stop.

"For heaven's sakes," she said. "Do you want to ruin your eyes?"

"What's the matter?" I asked. "I don't have any trouble seeing."

"I don't mean that," Mom replied. "I mean your eyes will look bloodshot in the photographs. Put that book down. Besides, I've got things to tell you."

So model time also became "Mom" time. Since my mother had quit her job at the office to be my manager, she ended up having a lot of time on her hands. In the mornings she slept a little later than usual, only getting up at nine to call the agency when they opened. After getting my schedule for the day, she would go to the supermarket and do odd jobs around the house until it was time to pick me up. Although she liked having the extra time, there wasn't anybody to talk to, like there used to be in the office. So when she came to pick me up, she insisted that I listen to her day while she drove me to New York.

"Why don't you work half days at the office?" I suggested one day. We were about to enter the Lincoln Tunnel, and Mom had just bored me with a detailed account of the laundry she had done.

"They won't allow it," Mom said. "And anyway, I'd be exhausted if I had to work all day and then take you to New York."

I didn't want to argue about that, so I let it pass. Anyway, it would've seemed silly to have Mom work half days for one hundred dollars a week when I could make nearly eight times that much. With that money I could pay for the food and rent and have plenty of money left over for college. If I could please my mother and my teachers and the agency, too, then life would be sure to be very pleasant for me.

And then there was Greg. I guess the reason I could get through school and work and still feel good was because I knew that on the weekends I was Greg's girl. Being with him was wonderful. On Saturdays we'd hang out with friends or go to the movies or talk about our writing. But we made Sunday morning our "wilderness" day. After being in school and New York all week, there was nothing I liked better than to put on a flannel shirt, an old pair of jeans, and hiking boots. I never put on makeup, and I let my hair hang free so I could feel it blowing around my neck in the spring breeze. The fresh air seemed to clear my pores of all the dirt and grime and heavy makeup of the preceding week, and it also felt like a sort of bath for my brain. When Greg and I were together on top of our mountain, I could feel all the pressures just melt away. Whenever he took me in his arms and kissed me under the bright blue sky, it felt like nothing else in the world was important: not school, not modeling, not even my mother. Then I wished Greg and I could build a cabin somewhere in the woods and live there forever. Of course, I knew it was all just a fantasy, but it sure felt good to think about it. At least on Sundays our dream could come true.

As long as school, modeling, and Greg remained three totally separate parts of my life, I could manage to handle them, even though it was tough having enough time for everything. But it wasn't so much the time that bothered me—it was the fact that I had to change identities for every role I played. For Mom I had to be a beautiful model-daughter. For my teachers I had to remain serious and studious. For Greg I had to be yet another person, a natural girl who never used makeup and preferred the simple outdoors life. With each different set of people, I was convinced I was who they thought I was at that moment, but then the time would come when I had to be somebody else again. It was almost enough to drive a girl crazy.

Yet it was spring, and just seeing all that life blossoming around me gave me energy, too. In just a matter of months, school would be out. Then I'd only have to be Greg's girl and Mom's daughter, and maybe I'd even have time left to be myself. I managed to keep my sanity by convincing myself that summer was sure to solve everything.

But about three weeks after I shot the *Miss* cover, the real trouble started. It was Saturday morning, and I was searching through my closet in search of the right outfit to wear to the April Fool's bash that evening. The dance was strictly informal; in fact, the object was to arrive in the most outrageous-looking clothes possible. I'd found the top I was looking for: a hideous, electric-orange print shirt I'd received from one of my California relatives. I was just beginning to hunt for an old pair of pants when Mom came up behind me.

"What are you doing, Renée?" She was holding a clothing box under her left arm. "Here, try this on."

"I'm getting together my outfit for tonight's April Fool's bash. Isn't this shirt a scream?" I said, holding it out for her inspection.

Mom tossed the shirt onto my bed. "Did you say tonight?" she asked, a trace of alarm in her voice. "Oh, Renée, I'm very sorry, but you're going to have to cancel your plans."

"Why, Mom? I've been looking forward to this dance for weeks."

"Sorry, dear. Business. There's a very important party tonight at Baker and Saterhorn. They're a very important agency—one of the best—and it's important they see you."

"But why tonight? I thought they had these things only during the week."

"I don't know why. The thing is we have to go. They're looking for a new girl to represent the Mary Bell cosmetics line, and Mrs. Floyde says they're very interested in you. If you make a good impression on them tonight, the job is practically in the bag."

"But, Mom—"

"No buts, Renée. You're going, and that's it. Here, try on this dress I got for you." She placed the box on top of my orange shirt and left the room.

Calling Greg that morning was one of the hardest things I've ever had to do. As I pushed the buttons of his number, I vowed to tell him the truth once and for all. But somehow, when I heard his sweet voice on the other end of the line, I couldn't go through with it.

"Hey, I didn't expect to hear from you so soon," Greg said cheerfully. "All set for tonight? Just wait till you see my getup."

"Greg, I—I have some bad news. . . . I can't make it tonight. You see, my mother—"

"Is she all right?" he asked, concerned.

"Well, um, not exactly. She's still real depressed about this job situation of hers, and I don't think it'd be a good idea for me to leave her alone tonight. She needs my company—I'm all she has, you know—"

"I'll come over, then, and we can make it a threesome," he suggested.

"No, I don't think that'd be a good idea," I said, trying to think of a reason why it wouldn't. "She, um, doesn't like to let anyone know how down she gets, so I think she'd feel better if it was just me."

"Well, if you insist," he said. I could tell he didn't quite believe me, but he didn't want to press the issue.

"Why don't you go on ahead to the bash? I want a complete detailed account of who wore what and what went on. I'll see you tomorrow, okay?"

"Okay," Greg said. "See ya."

Fortunately, when I saw him the next morning, things between us were as comfortable as they always were. Greg evidently had believed my lie after all. He brought over a bouquet of wild flowers for my mother. She was puzzled, but she accepted them and thanked him for his gesture. When we got up to our mountain, he gave me his play-by-play version of the bash, which had proved to be a success. At times I wanted to interrupt and tell him all about *my* party and how I'd charmed the account executives at Baker and Saterhorn, but I kept my silence. The time still wasn't right.

The calm of that Sunday afternoon was but a pleasant memory by Wednesday. At lunch Marilyn got mad at me for the umpteenth time because I had to study and refused to listen to her talk about her new boyfriend. "Now that you're a star, you have no time for the little people," she cried. "I hope it's worth it, big shot!"

Although I felt bad about it, I had neither the time nor the desire to run after her and patch things up. Besides, I had something more pressing on my mind. Since Mom had informed me that I had no appointments that afternoon, I'd invited Greg over after school. We planned to do some work on our essays, and I wanted to show Greg this new book I'd bought in New York. It was a photo essay of the Colorado Rockies that breathtakingly captured their beauty. I was sure Greg would love it.

Mom was out when we arrived, so I put together a snack of cheese and crackers for us and brought it up to my room.

We pored over the pages, our heads touching. After each turn of the page, Greg would lightly rest his fingers on my back. It felt so warm to have him close to me like that that I wished he could stay by my side forever.

"What's going on here?" Mom's sharp voice broke into our reverie.

"Oh, hi, Mom," I said, feeling embarrassed. "Greg and I were just looking at this book." I looked down at the picture of the longhorn sheep, figuring its haughty expression was better to look at than Mom's.

But she was too caught up in what she had to say to chastise me for bringing Greg into my room. "I've got great news. The agency call 1 this morning, and the Mary Bell deal is on. You're their model. The shoot is tomorrow morning. . . ."

I didn't respond and didn't even quite hear the rest of what she had to say. All I knew was that my little secret was a secret no longer.

"Renée, what's she talking about?" Greg's question was so inevitable I almost laughed.

But Mom spoke before I had a chance to react. "Surely, Greg, Renée's told you about her chance at becoming the new representative of Mary Bell cosmetics."

"Why, no, Mrs. Renshaw, she hasn't." Greg's measured words betrayed his increasing anger.

"Oops." Mom giggled. "Sorry I let the cat out of the bag." She tiptoed out of the room to leave us alone.

Mom had no way of knowing I'd never told Greg the truth—she'd naturally assumed I'd told the world about my new career.

"Greg, let me explain—"

"Explain what? That you lied to me? That's very evident," he spat out.

"But there's a good reason. You see—"

"I'm not interested in hearing your excuses. All that matters is that you lied to me!"

"Greg, you're being unreasonable."

"*I'm* being unreasonable?" he shouted. I'd never heard him raise his voice before, and the sound was harsh and ugly. "Whatever happened to our trust?"

"Nothing's happened. I love you, Greg."

"How do I know that? Here you are, obviously leading a secret life that you didn't want me to know about. You know I don't like secrets and game playing. How do I know you're not hiding anything else from me—like another guy?"

"Oh, don't be silly. You know there's no one else."

"Do I? I just don't know now, Renée. I don't trust you anymore." With that he stormed out of the room. Even from where I stood, I could hear the slam of the front door.

Numbly I walked to the full-length mirror on the back of my bedroom door. "I hate you," I spat at the image before me. "I hate being pretty. I wish I was ugly." Then I turned and threw myself across my bed, sobbing uncontrollably.

Chapter Ten

The next morning Mom got me up early and after I washed my hair, put on basic makeup, and had a quick breakfast of strawberries and yogurt, we were off. But my heart wasn't in it now that I'd lost Greg.

"Cheer up, honey," Mom said as we drove to New York. "You'll be able to straighten things out with Greg. Give him time."

"I don't know, Mom. He was pretty upset."

"He'll come around. Besides, I want you to put your thoughts on this booking. Next to your cover for *Miss*, it could be one of the most important jobs you could ever get."

"Why did they schedule this for the morning? I thought all my bookings were for after school."

"This is why this job is so important," Mom said excitedly. "This ad they're doing calls for an adult model. Once other companies see it, they'll want to hire you, too. It'll open up many doors that are closed to you right now."

"So why me? I'm only sixteen."

"But with the right makeup and hairstyle you can look twenty-two. The agency people saw that the other night. And the older you look the more jobs you can get."

"I see," I said glumly. Despite the importance of this job, I still felt miserable. What good was it to be a successful model if the boy I loved thought I was a complete phony?

We were in the throes of the rush-hour traffic, with cars, buses, and trucks squeezed in on us from all sides. Mom looked like she was going to be nervous about being on time again. She kept hitting the steering wheel every time we were forced to stop and looked like she was muttering some words under her breath.

But we were right on schedule. A few minutes before nine, we drove up to the building where the studio was located. As usual, it was on a dark side street of the city, where old, rundown warehouses loomed out as you passed them on the sidewalk. A couple of photographers had told me that these buildings contained the cheap, wide, lighted spaces they needed to hold all their equipment and have room to shoot. Still, I wished the area looked better. I always found myself imagining what the place looked like before the Dutch came to Manhattan and offered the Indians twenty-four dollars' worth of trinkets in order to wreck the place.

"By the way," Mom said, "the agency doesn't require me to accompany you on adult jobs, and since the weather's getting warmer, I decided that today would be a good time to go and buy the summer things you'll need. You can manage on your own, can't you?"

"Sure," I replied. "I have before, haven't I?" My doubts increased, however, as I glanced at the building. The lobby looked gloomy in the early morning light, and I was sure the elevator would choose today to get stuck.

"You know, on this job you might get a bonus fee. They may use the picture on a poster or billboard," Mom added.

I thought of what Marilyn had said about my picture being pasted on the huge billboard that hung over the baseball field at school. The thought made me cringe a bit at first, but on the other hand, it would be kind of neat. If it happened.

"I know," I said. "See you later." And then, since I was early, I watched as she drove away over the patched, pitted city street.

The blaring sound of rock music seemed

literally to hit me in the face when I pushed open the heavy door of Paul Mechant's studio a few minutes later. A man wearing jeans, a black T-shirt, and sneakers greeted me at the door. He was eating a cream donut, and the crumbs were sticking in his beard.

"*Bonjour, ma chérie.* How nice to see you," he said as he let the door slam behind him. "I'm Paul."

With that formality out of the way, he grabbed me in a big bear hug. From the way he acted, you would've thought we were long-lost brother and sister, instead of complete strangers. I recognized this as being one of the affectations of the business, and I went along with it dutifully. Inside, however, it gave me the creeps.

"Could you please turn the music down?" I asked, pulling away from him. He seemed annoyed by my request.

"But of course," he answered with false sweetness. "Anything for *ma petite lapine.*"

I hurried to the dressing room, hoping to find the makeup artist or somebody already there. But there was no one, so I put my model bag on the makeup counter, sat down, and began to unpack my things. The place had obviously been used heavily the day before. There was garbage everywhere. Discarded paper coffee cups lay dripping their last remains on the floor alongside tissues soiled with bright red lipstick smudges.

"Is that better?" I heard Paul's voice behind me. He had a slight accent—another affectation of the business, I suspected. He didn't look French to me.

"Thanks," I returned blandly. "Loud music in the morning makes me nervous."

"Such a serious young girl," Paul said. "Such a shame. At this time of your life, you should be having fun."

"I have fun," I said. "Do you know where I can plug in my hot rollers?"

"Right over there." He pointed to the outlet. "Most of my models love music," Paul persisted.

"I do love music," I said. "It's just a little early in the morning for me."

"Oh, early, early," he mocked me. "I just consider it a continuation of last night. You should too, *ma chérie.*"

Why should I? I wondered, but aloud I said, "Where's the makeup man?"

"What's the matter?" Paul smirked. "Relax. Enjoy the morning." He stood behind me now, touching my shoulders as I set my rollers up against the mirror. Already I didn't like him, and I wished Mom hadn't chosen today for me to go it alone. I could have used some of her overprotection.

Fortunately, at that moment we heard the metal door swing open. "Paul?" a male voice called.

"In the dressing room," Paul responded.

A moment later, a tall blond man walked jauntily into the room. From the large green tackle box he carried, I could tell he was the makeup artist. Paul embraced him just as he had me. But realizing this was just Paul's way didn't make me like him any better.

The young man walked over to where I sat and took off his coat, a thrift shop version of the old high school letter jacket. Paul introduced us.

"Johnny, meet a very serious girl, Renée Renshaw. She expects to make it in this business hating music." His loud laugh echoed off the stark white walls.

Johnny took the cue and tittered nervously. I could tell he wanted to please Paul, who obviously had hired him for the job.

Paul left to set up the lights, while Johnny began to pin my hair back in order to start my makeup.

"Paul's a great guy," he told me as he applied some creamy base to my skin. "Of course, he gets a little temperamental at times, like any artist. If you want to get along with him, you just have to laugh with him.

From the way the pictures come out, it's worth it. He's incredibly good."

"Uh-huh," I answered doubtfully. I wasn't convinced that acting like a jerk had anything to do with art, but if everybody else seemed to believe so, who was I to complain?

During the forty-five minutes Johnny spent doing my makeup, Paul came into the dressing room no less than ten times to check the results. He would put a stool down right next to me and stare down into my pores, just as if I were one of Mr. Brooks's microscopic specimens. It made me nervous to feel him so close to me, and I couldn't really tell him to go away. His beard still held some bits of cream from his donut, and looking at them made me sick to my stomach. But I had a job to do and tried to calm myself as best I could.

"No, no, no," he told Johnny after he came in and inspected me for the fourth time. "I'm never going to get this shot if you don't work a lot harder on that face. Renée needs all the help she can get."

I felt my body freeze. Was I supposed to shrug that off with a laugh? Paul had insulted me! What should I do? Scream? Call the agency? Leave? No, I couldn't do that—I was booked for the job, and everybody was depending on me to do it right. I was stuck.

As soon as the client walked in, Paul was sure to act nicer. Then I'd be able to relax.

"The client asked for a soft, natural look," Johnny protested sweetly, brushing some rouge over my cheekbones.

"Yeah, but she wants a *pretty* natural look, not a dees-gust-eeng one," Paul growled. Then he put a hand under my chin and held it hard. "Where in the world did you get that nose!"

"From my father," I said simply, trying to keep cool.

"Where ees he? I'll punch the jerk in the face."

"He's dead," I said flatly.

Paul didn't say a word but continued to scowl at Johnny.

"You're going to ruin my job," Johnny pleaded meekly. "Don't worry, Paul, I'll fix that nose up. I haven't put any contour powder on it yet, that's all."

"You'd better," said Paul, and then he returned to his set.

A few minutes later, three people walked in. One, a well-dressed woman carrying an attaché case, was the representative from Mary Bell cosmetics. A younger woman, wearing very baggy pants pulled stylishly tight at the waist, was her assistant. The man was the art director. He worked for the advertising agency that handled the Mary Bell line of cosmetics. A young boy, the photographer's assistant, also appeared suddenly out of the darkroom in the back of the studio. I breathed a sigh of relief. Maybe now Paul would treat me nicer, I hoped.

When Johnny finished my makeup, the woman client and her assistant came into the dressing room to tell me what to wear in the photograph. It turned out they wanted just a plain white bath towel, as my shoulders had to be bare in the picture. The woman from Mary Bell explained that nothing should detract from the face in a cosmetics shot.

After I sat down on the stool in front of the camera, Paul Mechant took a look at me through the camera. He was as grouchy as ever. "Pull that towel down!" he growled.

Cautiously I pulled the towel down a couple of notches and repositioned myself on the stool.

But he was far from satisfied. "I said pull that thing down!" he screamed.

Frightened, I looked around me for support, but everybody's face was blank. They didn't see anything wrong with his attitude. Only Johnny looked at me anxiously, but that was because he was checking my makeup.

Paul peered into the camera and then quickly brought his face around from back. In the sweetest little boy voice you ever heard, he said, "P-l-e-a-s-e, Miss-Sugar-and-Spice-and-everything-nice, *your towel is in my picture!*"

Everybody burst into laughter. No doubt they all thought he was the funniest guy in the world. I pulled the towel down a little lower and vowed that if he asked me to move it one more time I'd walk out of the studio, ad or no ad. I had never felt so miserable in my whole life. Did he think I was a stripper?

Finally the Polaroid pictures that Paul's assistant, Jay, had been taking to check the light quality proved successful, and Paul was ready to begin. Positioning himself behind the camera, he began to click the shutter and call out directions to me.

"Face up!" he yelled. "Now, turn to your right a smidge. No, no, I said a smidge. Put some expression into your face—no, not like that. I don't want kid stuff! Look at me like you mean it!"

Mean what? I thought. That I really hate your guts?

"I said look at me!" Paul growled. "Look at me like I am your boyfriend. You want to go out with me. Come on!"

For the life of me, I couldn't pretend I liked him. I tried hard to concentrate on Greg instead, but thinking about him only made me sad.

"Liven up, Renée," Paul yelled. "Give it to me. Show me your best."

Somehow, Paul managed to shoot a whole roll of film. As Jay was reloading the camera, Paul moved up close to me.

"I want more action, more expression," he boomed. "Let's try again. Turn up the music, Jay."

Jay obliged, and Paul continued to talk to me. But to me it sounded more like taunting. "Come on, Renée, sparkle. We don't have all day. Give me a smile. Look alive. Let go," he said as he clicked off a few more shots.

I couldn't figure out what I was doing wrong. Sensing Paul wanted me to work with the music, I tried to move my body to the hard, pulsing beat. But all he did was scowl. Then I stood still, striking a defiant pose that I thought made me look older. But that didn't seem to work right, either.

Nevertheless, Paul continued to push me. He wasn't friendly and genial, the way the other photographers I had worked with were. He was like an animal, hungry and impatient. And I was his prey.

"I want passion. I want a hot look. We're selling sex, Renée. Give me a hot look. You're a big girl now. Show me!"

"I don't know what you want," I cried, unable to take this man's taunts any longer. "Stop it! Stop it!" Grabbing the lower end of the towel, I bent over and tried to dab the tears from my eyes but wound up smearing the makeup instead.

"Oh, now look at the little girl," Paul sneered. "She's ruined the makeup." He made clucking sounds to show his contempt. "It's so sad, she had all the makings of a good one. Okay, let's wrap it up. No more shooting today. The little girl can't take it."

At that moment I didn't care about Mom or the agency or the client or the prestige and money this ad would have given me. All I knew was I had to get out of this place, out of this world that I wasn't old enough or mature enough to enter. I couldn't give Paul what he wanted because he was asking for something I just didn't have inside. I ran into the dressing room to get my things.

I hoped Mom would understand that this wasn't my fault; yet I couldn't be sure that she would. This whole modeling business had made a different person out of her. What if she were to think I goofed up on purpose?

The client's assistant came in just then to

put a few things into the bag she was carrying. She never once looked at me. She was soon followed by the client's representative, whose face looked cold and icy. "I'm sorry, but we're going to have to call your agency and tell them that you refused to cooperate with us."

"That's okay," was all I said. I didn't see any point in trying to convince her that I had really tried. It wouldn't have made any difference.

After she left to telephone the agency, Johnny came in. "Oh, my beautiful makeup job!" he wailed. Looking in the mirror, I noticed that my tears had smudged my mascara, and now I had two ugly black spots under my eyes. I stood meekly while he wiped off the makeup, and then I grabbed my things and left without a word. I did think I saw the art director give me a pitying look as I ran out the door, but I couldn't be absolutely sure.

Chapter Eleven

About one hour later, the old Ford pulled up to the littered curb where I stood waiting. I noticed piles of packages in the back seat of the car when I got in, and I knew they contained the stylish new clothes I was supposed to wear on all my spring appointments. Now I wondered if I'd even be going on any more calls after the agency found out what had happened.

"Why, Renée, you've been crying! What happened?" Mom exclaimed when I plopped dejectedly into the car.

I told her all about my booking with Paul Mechant, hoping with all my heart she'd understand.

"That awful man!" she gasped after I'd finished my story. "Wait until I tell Mrs. Floyde about him!" I noticed she had turned the car around, and instead of heading for the tunnel out of the city, she was driving back toward midtown.

"Where are you going?" I protested. "I thought you were going to take me to school."

"To the agency, of course!" Mom fumed. "I'm not letting anybody get away with treating you so crudely. We're going over there to tell them everything exactly the way you just told me."

"No, we're not, Mom," I said quietly but firmly.

"What?" Surprised, she looked at me.

"I don't want to go to the agency," I repeated. "Right now I want to go to school. You can talk to Mrs. Floyde yourself later. After all, you *are* my business manager."

Mom never said another word. But she turned around and drove me back to East-brooke.

After Mom dropped me off at the school parking lot, she sped off. The comfortable surroundings of the school campus were never so inviting, I thought. Since it was a breezy, warm day, dozens of kids had taken their lunch breaks outdoors. Most of them stood around in groups, either talking, taking in the sun, or admiring some of the cars the seniors had driven to school that morning. As I walked up to the school entrance, lugging my model bag over one shoulder, Joanie Hempstead and Roberta Stevens came running up to me. They were friends of friends of friends and normally didn't talk to me much, but now they seemed absolutely thrilled to see me.

"Renée!" they called. "How's it going?"

"Fine," I answered. "What's up?"

"I bet you just came back from the city," Joanie said breathlessly after they'd caught up with me.

"How did you know?" I asked.

Roberta opened her big blue eyes wide. "Oh, Renée, how exciting! Why didn't you tell us you're a model?"

As I looked at her, stunned, Joanie added, "I can't wait for the new issue of *Miss* to come out. I just can't believe it! Are you really going to be on the cover?"

"Yes," I said. "How did you know?"

Then I saw Marilyn standing over at the other end of the school parking lot, where the dogwoods were just coming into bloom. There were about ten or twelve girls standing with her, and they all looked over at me. Nobody waved or anything; they just stared at me as if I was some unapproachable celebrity.

"Marilyn told us!" Joanie gushed. "Oh, Renée, why didn't you tell us sooner? It's too exciting!"

111

"I guess I just didn't think of it," I lied. "It's really just a job to me."

"Oh, sure," they answered in unison. Leaving them looking surprised and breathless, I ducked out of sight into the school entrance.

The junior girls' locker room was located in the school basement, and when I got there I paused for a moment to collect my thoughts. After taking my schoolbooks out, I stashed my model bag in the back of my locker. Footsteps behind me made me whirl around. It was a freshman girl who looked vaguely familiar.

"Is this the junior girls' locker room?" she asked.

"You should know your way around Eastbrooke High by now," I told her. "School only started about seven months ago."

"Oh, I know my way around!" She laughed, showing white teeth. "It's just my way of getting to talk to you. You're Renée Renshaw, aren't you?"

"Yes," I admitted. "And who are you?"

"I'm Suzie Cassis," she said, shaking back her pretty blonde hair. "My sister Patty is in your class. She said you were a model?"

"Yeah," I said. More girls were starting to trickle into the locker room, and I wanted to leave. I'd hoped to get a chance to see Greg on his way to Lunch Two, to try to explain everything. But I could see I'd have trouble even making it to biology on time. Why did this news have to break today of all days?

Suzie reached into her bag and brought out a pen and pad. "May I have your autograph?" she asked.

"Autograph!" I repeated, disbelieving. "You don't mean that, do you?"

"Sure I do."

"But that's crazy. I'm just a girl like you. Not some movie star or something."

"But I want it," Suzie insisted. "I collect autographs. I've got over one hundred already—singers, actors, baseball players, everybody."

"So why me?"

"You'll be famous, that's why. Or at least well-known."

"Well, all right," I said reluctantly. I wrote my name in a big sprawl all over the pad she held out for me.

The bell rang just then, and after thanking me, Suzie disappeared out of the room. A heavy lump seemed to settle in my stomach. I felt betrayed by Marilyn. How could she have done such a thing? But then I remembered the times I'd hurt her feelings by being rude to her. I hadn't been much of a friend to her lately.

By the time I got into the hallway, time was

running short, and kids were scurrying along to their classes, bumping and jostling me in their efforts to get there on time. I tried to concentrate on the lab report Mr. Brooks was sure to ask for today, but no matter how I tried, my mind was one big blank. All I could think of was Paul Mechant and Marilyn and most of all, Greg.

Chapter Twelve

Anybody stopping in for a visit at 1318 John Street the next morning would've found two very depressed ladies sitting at breakfast. Mom and I tried hard to swallow our scrambled eggs, but they stuck to the roofs of our mouths like chewing gum. I was depressed because, after trying all night, I couldn't get through to Greg. His mother kept telling me he was out. Mom was still upset about what had happened at the studio.

"If I only had the nerve," Mom said, "I'd wring every one of their necks: Paul Mechant, the Mary Bell people, Mrs. Floyde and her stupid agency—everybody!"

"Take it easy, Mom," I said, patting her on the shoulder. "You told me once yourself, this whole business is based on luck."

"Luck, maybe," she answered despondently. "But not deceit. Why didn't Mrs. Floyde tell me that 'selling sex' was what the job was about? I never would have allowed you to do it if I had known."

"But that's not Mrs. Floyde's job. The company liked my look and wanted to use me. It was her job to send me over there. Nobody knew I wasn't ready for it."

"But she should have known—she's been in this business a long time." Mom continued to grumble, not even hearing what I had just said. "My God, you're only a child!"

"You're not listening, Mom," I nearly shouted at her. "You know how the modeling profession works. You're paid to do whatever the job calls for. If you can't do it, they just get someone else."

Mom looked at me with surprise. "My, my," she said. "You certainly have a much healthier attitude about this than I do."

"Well, it's not like I'm all washed up. The catalog people still like me. And that's where the real money is," I said.

"That's true. But that ad could have given you so much exposure."

I thought of Greg just then and how, even without the exposure, I had ruined his idea of the kind of girl I was. He'd probably never talk to me again, not after the way he'd reacted to me the other day.

"So you're not too upset about the ad?" Mom repeated.

116

She was wearing an old, faded flannel robe that was draped about her body in wrinkled, sloppy folds. Her hair was still uncombed, and since she hadn't yet put on any makeup, her face looked pale and drawn. Suddenly I found myself wishing she had her old job back at Stanford Plastics. At least then she had somewhere to go in the morning. But I knew there was little chance of that happening as long as I was still able to get work.

"I'm not too upset about that," I answered her. "Just upset about Greg."

Mom looked at me sympathetically. "I've taken you away from the things you should be concerned about—boys, your schoolwork, Marilyn. . . ." She sounded defeated.

"It's not your fault," I said, trying to cheer her up. But inside I wasn't so sure.

Chapter Thirteen

After homeroom I ducked into the girls' room for a minute to freshen up. I didn't put on any makeup, of course, but I wanted to comb my hair out long and shiny, the way Greg liked it. There was no way he could avoid me today. My plan was to corner him after English class and convince him I really was the same girl he knew and loved. Because I *was* still that same girl. Then I made a tough decision: if Greg still couldn't accept me, I would have to forget him, no matter how much it hurt. I had to be myself first.

"Be yourself, be yourself," I kept coaching myself as I stood brushing my hair in front of the mirror. But as hard as I tried to convince myself I could forget Greg, I knew I really couldn't. If he left me or found another girl, I would simply die. I'd probably lose so much weight that I'd be too skinny to model. Then Mom would have to go back and work at

Stanford Plastics whether she liked it or not.

The door to the bathroom swung open just then. It was Marilyn, who looked at me curiously for a moment. Then she spoke up.

"Hey, Renée, congratulations!" I noticed that she was holding the new issue of *Miss* magazine. It was the first time I'd seen it, and it gave me quite a jolt to see my smiling face on the cover.

"I'm glad I found you," she continued. "You did a terrific job." She seemed honestly happy for me.

"Let me see." I took the magazine from Marilyn's outstretched hand. They had decided to use the picture of me in the shorts outfit, and I had to admit I liked the way it turned out. I looked just like every girl's idea of the happy, well-adjusted teen. I thought of the millions of girls who'd look at me and wish they were in my place. Little would they know that this pert-looking girl was slowly dying of a broken heart.

"I'm really proud of you," Marilyn continued. "I guess you're pretty mad I let the word out, though."

"No, the whole school's probably seen this or will soon. Besides, I have been treating you pretty crummy lately."

"That's true. You're a conceited, self-centered, narcissistic drip!"

"Oh, yeah? Well you're a loud-mouthed, hotheaded tattletale!"

We looked at each other for a second, then burst out laughing. Impulsively I grabbed her and gave her a quick hug. "I'm glad I have a friend like you."

Feeling a little better about myself, I ran down the hall to make it to class before the late bell rang.

Mrs. Milton began class by announcing, "There are a number of you who have catching up to do on your English assignments. So we're not going to have a regular class today. I want you to use the time to finish up your assignments."

Good, I thought. I'd have a chance to get some work done on my essay. As I opened my notebook, Mrs. Milton said, "Renée, I'd like to talk to you."

Reluctantly I got up and walked to her desk. I knew what this was about.

"I'd like you to give me your first draft of the essay for the contest," she told me point-blank.

"I don't have one," I admitted, surprised at how good it felt to say that. Even while I waited, agonized, for Mrs. Milton's stunned reaction, I was glad to have it out.

But she didn't seem the least bit angry. "I heard you've been very busy lately," she said.

"Oh, Mrs. Milton!" I exclaimed. "That's really an understatement. You should hear what's been going on lately."

And then, very quickly, I told her everything—about my mother, the modeling, Paul, and Greg.

"Want to write about it?" she asked after I'd finished.

Puzzled, I looked at her.

"You know," she said, "write about the experiences you've been having, just as you told them to me."

I looked at her doubtfully. "You really think so?"

"My dear," she said, "it's obvious from what you said that you've been under quite a strain. But you've still been able to keep up your activities. It's a remarkable story of determination and responsibility."

"But there's so little time left."

"There's time enough. You can start working on it now. In fact, why don't you go over this with Greg? He can help you get it into shape." Before I could say a word, she said, "Greg Neill, please come up here."

Greg stood and walked over to Mrs. Milton's desk. He avoided looking at me. Mrs. Milton said, "Greg, Renée needs help on her essay. I want you to work on it with her this period.

Renée, I expect to see a first draft on Monday."

Reluctantly Greg followed me to the back of the room. I could tell this was the last place in the world he wanted to be right now, but I was grateful to Mrs. Milton for giving me the chance to explain everything to him.

"Greg," I began. "I know you think I betrayed you—"

"Boy, that's an understatement," he growled.

"Hear me out. You know only half the story. There *is* a reason why this nature girl has entered the great big artificial world of modeling."

I began by explaining the situation with my mother, how I had to do it for her and how I was afraid to tell him the truth.

When I finished telling him my story, I noticed that a film had formed over his clear blue eyes. He didn't say a word. I wasn't sure whether he truly believed me.

"You had every reason to be disgusted with me," I insisted. "You saw that I wasn't the person you thought I was. I don't blame you for being angry."

Greg said slowly, "I guess I did make it hard for you to be honest. Me, with my ideas about wholesomeness and beauty. I never gave you a chance to explain."

I stood there for a moment staring at him, feeling stunned. I wanted so badly to hold him and be held and to feel his kisses on my lips the way I had before.

"I love you, Greg," I whispered in his ear, so no one else could hear.

"I love you too, Renée," he said, and the big smile on his face told me it was true.

"I wish I could've been there at the shooting with Paul Mechant," Greg murmured. "I would never have let him treat you like that. I just can't imagine it."

"He was just doing his job," I said. "He has a crude way of doing it, that's all. Besides, I'm a big girl now. I should be able to handle things like that myself."

Greg looked at me lovingly. "I guess you are," he agreed. "You know, Renée, you really are wonderful. I bet your mom's real proud of you."

I let that pass. "I'm okay," I joked. "But I like you better."

Chapter Fourteen

Greg and I made a date for that very night at his house so that we could get the first draft of my essay done. We figured that if we worked hard, we could get it done over the weekend. On Monday Mrs. Milton could go over it, and we could still make the contest deadline, which was two weeks away.

The only problem was my mother. No doubt she wouldn't want me staying out late over the weekend. She had said something about a heavy day of appointments with photographers and clients on Monday, to keep the momentum up before anyone heard about my Mary Bell fiasco. Thinking about it, however, I made a firm decision: Greg and the essay were very important to me—as important as my modeling was to her. For the time being, modeling would have to take a back seat. Right now I had a lot of living to catch up on.

There would be plenty of time to model in the summer.

When I got back home later that afternoon, I resolved to have a long talk with my mother and let her know how I really felt about things. I was going to make some important demands, such as more time to spend on school and myself. She would just have to understand that I would make up the lost income on vacations.

But Mom was nowhere to be found. The car was gone, too, and she hadn't left a note explaining her absence. The breakfast things were still on the table, just the way we'd left them that morning. Needless to say, the scrambled eggs had turned into little balls of yellow rubber, and the morning coffee had stained the cups black. As I cleared the dishes off the table and put them into the sink, I noticed something lying discarded on the floor. It was my mother's robe. Obviously, something had happened this morning soon after I left for school to make her pick right up and leave the house as if it were on fire. Only the house was fine. Something had happened with Mom, and I didn't know what it could be.

At five-thirty I made myself a hasty dinner of tuna salad and got ready to go over to

Greg's house. My mother still hadn't returned yet, and I knew that in this case leaving a note wouldn't be enough. What if something terrible had happened to her? Maybe it was best to call Greg and just cancel our date for tonight again.

Then at quarter to six I heard the key turn in the front door. It occurred to me that this was exactly the time Mom used to return home, and for a second I felt very confused. Something felt very right at the same time that it felt wrong.

"Renée, honey," I heard her call me. "Are you home?"

"Right here, Mom," I yelled back from the kitchen. "What happened? I was worried about you. The place was a mess, and I thought—"

Suddenly she stood before me, and I had to suppress a gasp. Mom was wearing a two-piece business suit, a bright lavender summer linen. In her right hand she carried an attaché case, and on her face was a great big smile.

"I'm back at Stanford," she announced proudly.

For a second I was speechless. Then I burst out, "Mom, you didn't have to do that for me! I know how much you hated working there. I don't mind modeling, I really don't!"

"This doesn't have anything to do with your modeling," she began. "Though the events of the past few days have made me realize I haven't been pulling my own weight around here."

"But, Mom," I protested, though without much conviction, "you hated working as a secretary. I don't mind supporting us, really I don't. Anyway, you put in your share of the work."

Mom walked over to me and kissed my forehead. "I pushed you into a situation you weren't ready for. It was wrong. Anyway, I'm not a secretary anymore.

"Sitting here this morning I realized I missed the office. I sucked in my pride and called Stanford, asking for my old job back. They said no—but that there was a job open in sales. I had an interview today with the sales director. He thought that with my knowledge of the company and my experience as your manager, I'd make a good sales representative. He offered me the job on the spot!" She put her attaché case on the table and smiled. "It means a big salary hike for me, too, Renée."

I flung my arms around her neck and gave her the biggest congratulatory kiss you ever heard. "Oh, Mom, that's wonderful."

"You don't have to model now if you don't

want to," she added. "We'll be able to make it on what I'll bring in."

That was the best news of all. "Mom, I'd like to stay and help you celebrate your new job, but there's a boy I've been neglecting lately who I've promised to see now."

"You mean Greg?" she said. "Go have a good time. And, Renée," she added, "ask him if he'll forgive a nearsighted old mother who'd taken leave of her senses for a while."

A few minutes later I arrived at Greg's house. For a fleeting second I couldn't help but imagine Mrs. Floyde's horrified reaction to my appearance: hair parted in the middle and hanging straight down my back, no makeup, and wearing old Levi's, sneakers, and a green plaid flannel shirt. The last thing in the world I looked like was a glamorous model.

But I looked just fine to Greg, whose friendly smile as he led me inside told me more than words ever could that I was still his girl.

"I brought a little present," I said, handing him a small brown paper bag.

"What is it?" he asked.

"Look inside."

Greg opened the bag and took out one of the oatmeal granola cookies I'd baked that afternoon. "Umm, these are pretty good," he said. "I didn't know you knew how to bake."

Grabbing the bag from his hand, I reached in for a cookie and, to Greg's surprise, began to munch away happily.

"I thought models were supposed to watch their weight," he said.

"I told you these cookies are a present. They're to celebrate my retirement from the modeling business."

"But, Renée—your mother. Hey, you didn't quit because of me, did you?"

"No, Greg. I quit because of me. I need the time for myself right now. Besides, it's only for a little while—I'm going back to it this summer. From now on I'm going to control my modeling career, not have it control me."

Greg grinned. "You know, I still can't picture you prancing about under all those lights."

"There's a lot about me you still have to learn," I said suggestively. "Come on, let's get to work on my essay."

Chapter Fifteen

About a month later I ran into Patty Cassis' little sister Suzie on my way to school.

"Hi!" she called out when she saw me.

"Hi!" I returned. "How's the autograph business?"

"Fine," she said.

"I'll bet you threw out my autograph by now." I laughed.

"Why would I do a dumb thing like that?" she asked. By now we had entered the school grounds, and I could already see a group of kids gathering outside the entrance.

"Well, you know I've temporarily retired from modeling."

"It doesn't matter, you're still a neat girl."

Yes, I suppose I am, I thought, walking slowly toward the school. For some reason I chose that moment to turn around and gaze at the billboard facing the school athletic grounds. Plastered on it was a huge, monster-sized photograph of the girl who had replaced me as the symbol of Mary Bell cosmetics. "I hope it was worth it to you," I said to her face. "You may have glamour and success, but I've got something far more special." Smiling, I made my way toward Greg, who was waiting for me at the back entrance.

You'll fall in love with all the Sweet Dream romances. Reading these stories, you'll be reminded of yourself or of someone you know. There's Jennie, the *California Girl*, who becomes an outsider when her family moves to Texas. And Cindy, the *Little Sister*, who's afraid that Christine, the oldest in the family, will steal her new boyfriend. Don't miss any of the Sweet Dreams romances.

☐	22683	**SECRET IDENTITY #22** Joanna Campbell	$1.95
☐	22840	**FALLING IN LOVE AGAIN #23** Barbara Conklin	$1.95
☐	22957	**THE TROUBLE WITH CHARLIE #24** Jaye Ellen	$1.95
☐	22543	**HER SECRET SELF #25** Rhondi Villot	$1.95
☐	24292	**IT MUST BE MAGIC #26** Marian Woodruff	$2.25
☐	22681	**TOO YOUNG FOR LOVE #27** Gailanne Maravel	$1.95
☐	23053	**TRUSTING HEARTS #28** Jocelyn Saal	$1.95
☐	24312	**NEVER LOVE A COWBOY #29** Jesse Dukore	$2.25
☐	24293	**LITTLE WHITE LIES #30** Lois I. Fisher	$2.25
☐	23189	**TOO CLOSE FOR COMFORT #31** Debra Spector	$1.95
☐	23190	**DAYDREAMER #32** Janet Quin-Harkin	$1.95
☐	23283	**DEAR AMANDA #33** Rosemary Vernon	$1.95
☐	23287	**COUNTRY GIRL #34** Melinda Pollowitz	$1.95
☐	23338	**FORBIDDEN LOVE #35** Marian Woodruff	$1.95
☐	23339	**SUMMER DREAMS #36** Barbara Conklin	$1.95
☐	23340	**PORTRAIT OF LOVE #37** Jeanette Noble	$1.95
☐	23341	**RUNNING MATES #38** Jocelyn Saal	$1.95
☐	23509	**FIRST LOVE #39** Debra Spector	$1.95
☐	24315	**SECRETS #40** Anna Aaron	$2.25
☐	23531	**THE TRUTH ABOUT ME AND BOBBY V. #41** Janetta Johns	$1.95
☐	23532	**THE PERFECT MATCH #42** Marian Woodruff	$1.95

Prices and availability subject to change without notice.

TEENAGERS FACE LIFE AND LOVE

Choose books filled with fun and adventure, discovery and disenchantment, failure and conquest, triumph and tragedy, life and love.

☐	23796	**CHRISTOPHER** Richard Koff	$2.25
☐	23844	**THE KISSIMMEE KID** Vera and Bill Cleaver	$2.25
☐	23370	**EMILY OF NEW MOON** Lucy Maud Montgomery	$3.50
☐	22605	**NOTES FOR ANOTHER LIFE** Sue Ellen Bridgers	$2.25
☐	22742	**ON THE ROPES** Otto Salassi	$1.95
☐	22512	**SUMMER BEGINS** Sandy Asher	$1.95
☐	22540	**THE GIRL WHO WANTED A BOY** Paul Zindel	$2.25
☐	24143	**DADDY LONG LEGS** Jean Webster	$2.25
☐	20910	**IN OUR HOUSE SCOTT IS MY BROTHER** C. S. Adler	$1.95
☐	23618	**HIGH AND OUTSIDE** Linnea A. Due	$2.25
☐	20868	**HAUNTED** Judith St. George	$1.95
☐	20646	**THE LATE GREAT ME** Sandra Scoppettone	$2.25
☐	23447	**HOME BEFORE DARK** Sue Ellen Bridgers	$1.95
☐	13671	**ALL TOGETHER NOW** Sue Ellen Bridgers	$1.95
☐	20871	**THE GIRLS OF HUNTINGTON HOUSE**	$2.25
☐	23680	**CHLORIS AND THE WEIRDOS** Kin Platt	$2.25
☐	23004	**GENTLEHANDS** M. E. Kerr	$2.25
☐	20474	**WHERE THE RED FERN GROWS** Wilson Rawls	$2.50
☐	20170	**CONFESSIONS OF A TEENAGE BABOON** Paul Zindel	$2.25
☐	14687	**SUMMER OF MY GERMAN SOLDIER** Bette Greene	$2.25

Prices and availability subject to change without notice.

Buy them at your bookstore or use this handy coupon for ordering: